BLADESTRIKE

BLADESTRIKE

Chris Crowther

Bladestrike

Published by Wheatmark®
610 East Delano Street, Suite 104
Tucson, Arizona 85705 U.S.A.
www.wheatmark.com

International Standard Book Number: 978-1-58736-773-1
Library of Congress Control Number: 2006940826

PROLOGUE

Moonlight bathed the castle walls, its cloudless beams casting elongated shadows across the gravelled yard. In these islands of darkness a figure moved.

He was a tall man but on this Edwardian summer night his military bearing was stooped by taut nerves that received another jolt as, high above, the mournful bell of the tower clock struck the first hour of a new twenty-four. Time to move. He dug deep into his soul for resolution and coat pocket for the keys.

Ah, those keys; what duplicity getting them: his lover had obtained the originals, he had arranged the copies, the originals had been returned. Now to use them but, a hundred yards away in the flickering gaslit columns at the base of the tower, other figures were moving.

Over the weeks he had watched and timed the movements of soldier sentries and castle police and knew they were as ineffective to determined evasion as they were predictable. Hours ago, Detective Kerr would have completed his rounds and doubtless eventually swear that he had found all well. And so he would for perhaps many a night yet before they finally discovered.... he forced himself back to reality and watched the sentries abandon their posts and slip around the side of the building as they did every night. So much for a peacetime army. As a match flared on the east side of the tower and cigarettes glowed, he smiled and edged closer to the front door.

It was solid and heavy but only as strong as the locks that held it and closed only to those without a key. He selected one of the copies, slid it into the lock and turned. Seconds later the door was slightly ajar and he was sliding through and just as quietly closing it behind. He was in.

He knew this building, had spent many a day and not a few riotous nights within its grand walls and become a familiar figure to staff and guards alike. Now, with ghostly moonlight piercing the sash windows and sensing the darkness of his deed, its atmosphere was malevolent. Taking an extra deep breath and a tighter grip on the keys, he forced himself on, through the portico and circular hallway with its spiralling grand staircase and into a smaller hallway. To the left was the door to the strongroom. He passed it by and instead went through the door to his right: the library.

In the blue lunar light the rows of leather-bound boredom looked down on heavy furniture, plush carpets and ....the safe. It stood just offside of centre of the outside wall, smallish, ordinary and pitifully inadequate for its contents. He felt another quickening of the pulse, not from fear this time but excitement, like those nights on the veldt when his body trembled with the thrill of imminent action and daring deeds.

And what deed could be more daring than this? What would his fellow officers think if they could see him now? They had cast him out of his last regiment for one uncontrollable weakness and the bitterness still burned within him. But tonight would be a reckoning, make him rich and even a hero of sorts again but an anonymous hero for they must never know who'd done this. Perhaps they'd guess but they must never *know*. He selected another key and went to the safe.

TEN MINUTES AND THE contents were in his pocket and he was walking out, in his euphoria, even forgetting to lock the safe and main door behind him. It mattered little. The sentries were still absent from their posts as he marched briskly down the side of the yard not even worrying unduly if he was spotted: officers from outlying units were frequent visitors to the castle garrison and tonight he would be one of many exiting the front gate. Passing under the archway, he returned the 'present arms' of the sentries with a casual salute and an inward sigh. He was out.

Beyond the gate, across the cobbles glistening under the

gaslights, the usual line of horsecabs waited. He quickened his pace towards them, elation welling, relief pouring. He had entered one of the most fortified buildings in the kingdom and done the unthinkable.

The cabby's whip cracked, horseshoes clacked on the cobbles and a country's heritage disappeared into the night.

CHAPTER ONE

THE BELL 206 JET Ranger helicopter is a great bit of kit. Its 420 horsepower turbine can hover it over a spot or scoot along at a good hundred knots. Between the two it can fly at any old speed you want which comes in handy when the weather's lousy with low cloud, low visibility and rain. That's when you drop the lever, slow right down and hug the deck with the demisters screaming, tongue in cheek and eyes wide open for any masts and wires that would ruin your whole day.

It's probably not a very scientific way to operate in this high-tech age but when the chips are down there's still a lot to be said for scud-running. It's hard on the nerves, bad on range and doesn't exactly endear you to livestock farmers and the Civil Aviation Authority but it does get you there and getting there was what it was all about that wet and windy November morning.

My name's Mike Tempest. I've been to a few places, done a few things and flying helicopters was what I'd done most. I'd built a fair amount of experience over the years and perhaps a bit of skill and I certainly needed it now as I ground my way through that hell-awful weather. Not for the first time in my life I asked myself what I was doing there and why? I knew the answer this time: I'd been suckered into it by that stroppy little bitch at Tower Hill and I wouldn't even have met her if I hadn't gone into Ashmond's office and heard him say those magic words.

'YOU'RE FIRED TEMPEST'

Captain Ashmond was my Chief Pilot and not number one on my list of favourite people. *HELIJETS* was a four helicopter outfit operating from Denbridge, a grass airfield on the western edge of London. Small as our operation was,

Ashmond liked to think he was running some international conglomerate and his desk was part of the fantasy. I sat down opposite its varnished mahogany expanse.

'Really; why?'

Actually I knew the answer: our flying was mainly stroking the egos of yuppies from the city but fluctuations in the economy meant many were down to their last millions and expensive helicopter transportation was first for the chop with me just a number somewhere down the chain. Not that Ashmond needed much of an excuse; he and the other two pilots had all served together in the Queens Bengal Helicopter Lancers or some such outfit and taking me on when they were short of pilots had been a constant thorn in his regimental side. Giving me the heave-ho was almost an act of exorcism.

'You just don't fit in here, Tempest, you never have and you never will.' He settled himself back in his super-reclining chair. 'Your bush-flying ways might have gone down well in the Third World but they're hardly appropriate in executive aviation.'

I pulled a cigarette and lit up. Ashmond hated smoking in his office.

'So, I'm out on my ear.'

Ashmond waved away some smoke that was invading his personal airspace.

'Yes, and with immediate effect. The chairman's quite adamant. Standard redundancy payment will be in the post.' He glanced dismissively doorwards. 'Sandra will take care of details. Goodbye, Tempest.'

There are times when you have to bite you tongue and stay nice and leaving a job is one of them; you never know when you might be able to come back. So I just stubbed my cigarette on Ashmond's lovely desk, said 'Well stuff you, your chairman and your job', kicked my chair into the corner and door-slammed out.

'Oh Mike, how could you?' A slim girl with a thatch of close-cropped blonde hair was standing by the filing cabinet with a sad expression. Sandra was secretary, receptionist, booking officer and operations manager rolled into one and as big an asset to *HELIJETS* as its helicopters standing outside. Unbeknown to Ashmond, we'd got pretty close over the last months and I'd promised to take her out for a Chinese this evening. A great girl was Sandra even if her ethics stopped short of listening at the boss's door.

'Could what? He did it to me.' I gave a poor imitation of a smile. 'Sorry, Sandra, but you'll have to take a rain-check on tonight's supper. I need to sort things out. I'll give you a call.'

'I understand.'

She probably did too, knowing Sandra, but at the moment I neither knew nor cared as I stomped out to my old banger, gunned a bootful of revs and wheelspun off Denbridge airfield for what I thought was the last time.

Who needs a job anyway?

I DID AND QUICK if my dwindling bank balance was anything to go by. My small basement pad was never going to feature in *HELLO* magazine but my severance pay from *HELIJETS* wouldn't run it for long and already bills were coming in. Mid-November wasn't the best time to start looking for a flying job but I dragged out my list of contact numbers and got calling.

The helicopter world is small and the jungle drums quick to beat and their message this time wasn't hard to guess: Tempest is bad news. No-one actually said that but two days of ringing around while the whisky level fell in inverse proportion to my phone bill produced only 'get in touch' promises that were as unlikely as they were insincere.

The weather didn't help either. High pressure over the British Isles had enshrouded the capital in freezing fog that clawed at my windows like the creditors soon to come. With anti-cyclonic gloom outside and in, I was getting desperate. That's when the phone rang.

'Captain Tempest?' The voice was female, cool and businesslike to the point of brusque.

'That's me; who's that?'

'You don't know me, Captain Tempest, but I'm calling to offer you some work. You are available at the moment, I understand?'

'I've just been given the sack if that's what you mean. What sort of executive position are you offering?'

She gave a barely audible sigh just to show that my sarcasm wasn't appreciated.

'Not a position, Captain Tempest; work, just one day's work. If you're interested we can meet in town and discuss the proposal in more detail.'

This obviously wasn't going to provide for my old age but it could lead elsewhere and inject some interest into a so-far excruciatingly boring week.

'Okay; where and what time?'

'Tower Bridge. There's a cafe down at bank level on the northwest side. They've got some outside tables. Meet me there at ten a.m. tomorrow.'

'I'll be there.'

I hung up. No need to ask for a description; there wouldn't be too many punters sitting at outside tables this time of year. Besides, I wanted to show Miss Business Efficiency that I could cut the small talk just as sharply as her.

Perhaps I'd cut it too much; what was I getting into here and who was this extremely self-assured little madam? I tried a call-back but the number was ex-directory.

I hadn't even got her name.

CHAPTER TWO

NEXT MORNING THE UNDERGROUND rattled down to Tower Hill and disgorged me blinking into a morning bright and clear. Like me, the weather systems had tired of days of lethargic inactivity, shunted around in the Atlantic and given us a night of good clearing rain. The only remnant of yesterday was the cold, still stiletto sharp on an easterly wind straight from Siberia.

With minutes to go, I wandered anti-clockwise round the Tower. It was well out of season but there were still some tourists braving the river air and whirring away with VCRs. The sun and wind were invigorating and under the closed spans of the bridge, a string of tug-hauled barges were passing down-river. The days of the big ships in the Pool of London were long gone and the spans seldom opened these days. I compared the bridge to my own situation: years of intensive operation and then no longer needed. Well, there might still be use for me yet. I moved on to the café to find out just what.

Snuggling at the base of the bridge's northwest approach, it had a disconsolate air with metal tables and stacked chairs mirrored in puddles of last night's rain. Just one table was in use, a central one occupied by a lone figure huddled in the upturned collar of a fawn trenchcoat.

She stood up as I approached, a slender woman in her late thirties who still deserved to be called a girl. Short auburn hair framed a tastefully composed assembly of clear blue eyes, ringed ears, lean jaw and a well-proportioned mouth lacking only a smile. She glanced at her watch.

'To the minute, Captain Tempest.'

'It's how I try to operate.' It was ice-breaking time and I held out my hand, 'Call me Mike.'

Well-manicured fingers emerged from the trenchcoat pocket. They were unringed and surprisingly warm to the touch.

'For the sake of formality you can call me Miss Bird.'

The hand returned very deliberately to the pocket and she to her chair with straight-backed grace. One shiny-booted leg crossed the other as she looked me up and down.

'Do you always attend interviews dressed like some refugee from *Biggles*?'

I ignored the question, turned up the fur collar of my old flight jacket and nodded towards the café interior.

'Why the arctic survival exercise? Let's go inside and grab ourselves some coffee?'

Miss Bird remained immobile.

'We'll stay here where we can talk. If you'd care to go and collect you'll find two cappuccinos already paid for.'

With my ice-breaking talents seemingly on a par with the *TITANIC*, I went and collected, wishing I'd never mentioned the damn coffee and angry at being manipulated so easily. A wily little vixen was our Miss Bird. Inside the cafe a scattering of tourists reloaded their cameras and chatted away in unintelligible Nippon. There was no-one here to compromise confidentiality but Miss Bird was taking no chances. With only minor scalding I got the inevitable plastic cups back to our table and sat down.

'So, what's this job?'

'Not job, work, some freelance flying; are you interested?'

'I'm interested but I need to know more.'

She took a token unsugared sip of her cappuccino, leaned forward and fixed me with the piercing eyes of a lady who knew how to say no and probably did quite often.

'Later. First things first, Captain Tempest; can you provide a helicopter?'

I leaned forward in deliberate imitation.

'Probably. What sort of helicopter, how many people and for how long?'

She sat back.

'Something with good performance: Bell 206 or Hughes 500. Just you and two pax for one day.'

She knew her helicopters, this girl, and with the present dearth of punters there were plenty of spare ones sitting around, even *HELIJETS* if I played it right. I took out a cigarette and fired up.

'No problem; what's the operation?'

A shaft of wind blew in off the river rippling the coffee and her hair.

'Simple enough: fly to first location, pick up two pax, on to second, a minute on ground then final location and drop off pax. About two and a half hours flying total.' She leaned forward again. 'Could you handle that?'

'Of course I *can*.' Smoking is undoubtedly bad for the health but it does give you seconds to pause and think before opening your big fat mouth. She'd used the aviation term *"pax"* for passengers; Miss Bird had chartered aircraft before or at least worked around them. I blew a cloud of blue smoke across the table. 'The question is *will* I? Why ask me? Why not just go to one of the half-dozen heli-outfits around London and get yourself a machine and pilot off the shelf?' I took a swig of my coffee. 'What's this all about?'

The smoke cloud disintegrated immediately in the wind but she grimaced and fanned her hand anyway just to show what she thought of my filthy habit. A cup of coffee gives you thinking time too and she studied hers for a few seconds before looking up smiling. It was a mirthless smile but it still suited her.

'Captain Tempest, this is a job that requires some delicacy and my client requires absolute confidentiality. A regular operator would require times, places and, worst still, names. From you we can demand discretion. On top of that we would expect you to be more flexible with regard to weather minima and other restrictions that would inhibit an Air Operator Certificated company. For that we're prepared to pay well.'

'How well?'

'Two thousand pounds....cash.'

It was my turn to smile.

'Miss Bird, you're a smooth-talking little devil and you've talked me into it....almost.'

'Almost?'

'I want three thousand.'

She cocked her head in disgust.

'Ridiculous.'

A cloud passed over the sun and the river lost some of its twinkling sparkle. I stubbed the butt of my cigarette in the cheap tin ashtray.

'Listen, Miss Bird, this whole business stinks of being about as phony as your name. Okay, don't tell me the facts because I'd rather not know and as far as I'm concerned this will be just another job but it's still going to cost you....three thousand up front.'

By her side was a smart leather briefcase. She thought for a moment and then brought the case to the top of the table, twirled the combinations, flicked the locks and produced three buff envelopes.

'Twenty-five hundred, Tempest, and that's final.' One by one she threw the envelopes across the table. 'Fifteen hundred now and the balance on completion.'

I slit the envelopes and glanced inside: ten fifties in each. Jobless and broke isn't the best base for negotiation. I stuck the cash into the inside pocket of my flight jacket.

'Okay, you got yourself a pilot, Miss Bird; now tell me where I'm going and when.'

'First thing next Tuesday, so you've got plenty of time to organize your helicopter.' She reached again into the briefcase, brought out an Ordnance Survey map and tossed it across. Sheet 132 - Northwest Norfolk. 'Your first pickup will be somewhere on there. Your pax will direct you on to the next two points. I'll call you Monday evening and give you the grids for the first pickup. Don't discuss this with *anyone*....' she paused to make sure the emphasis on the last word had sunk in, '....any questions?'

'Just one: who put you on to me?'

Another of those mirthless little smiles flashed just long enough for me to see fine even teeth.

'I just looked around for some dumb bastard greedy enough for a number like this and somehow your name kept coming up.' She closed the lid of her case and clicked the locks leaving me wondering how many more of those little buff envelopes could have been negotiated by a dumb bastard not quite greedy enough. 'One more thing, Tempest....'

The tone of her voice brought me back out of the case.

'Yeh?'

'There's no going back on this now. You be at that pickup come hell or high water. No crap about weather or unserviceable aircraft. You *be* there.'

I nodded and lit another cigarette.

'I'll be there....and the name's Mike, remember.'

The smile glided back and this time it had just the faintest whiff of sincerity.

'Okay...Mike...seeing as you're now so flush with cash, you can go and buy me another coffee.'

I went and joined the queue again. Did I really want this... any of it? So far I'd always managed to control my life but now it seemed to be controlling me. Then I thought about those thirty facsimiles of Sir Christopher Wren nestling in my pocket and decided we all have to take a bit of agro sometime.

Outside the sky was clouding with the threat of more rain. I saved myself further scalding and boot leather by choosing a nearer table. There was no point in struggling to the old one because it was empty: Miss Bird had flown, coffee untasted, departure unobserved and trail untailed.

I drank my coffee quickly and left myself. Today was Thursday; less than three working days to talk some operator into sub-leasing me a helicopter. I patted the little buff envelopes again. No problem. Next Tuesday they'd be snuggling next to their brothers.

Or so I thought.

• • •

THROUGH THE RAIN SPLATTERED windshield, the gently undulating terrain of North Norfolk was reduced to a depressing
rain-soaked grey. At almost zero feet, I was having to undu-
late with it because, as forecast, the weather had deteriorated
dramatically enroute. With slivers of stratus ghosting past my
side windows, I trucked northwards and counted off the last
remaining miles.

Thankfully, there weren't many of them and I knew that
for sure because one advancement in recent years had made
the crude technique of scud-running infinitely easier: the
Global Positioning System. On top of my instrument panel
was a little black box that feasted on a gaggle of satellites
rotating somewhere out there in un-weathered space. With
Miss Bird's co-ordinates duly programmed, its inbuilt computer now showed course to fly, distance to run, groundspeed
and the time I'd actually get there. All I had to do for my
money was fly the aircraft but the weather was ensuring no
discounts.

I'd lifted off early from Denbridge and straight-lined out
but by halfway, heavy rain and clouds in the treetops had me
S-turning along an increasingly meandering track. This all
took time, fuel and money not to mention years off my life.
With the GPS now showing just two nautical miles to run I
held the cyclic tight and my breath through gritted teeth as
the barely-distinguishable ground features slid by in an enveloping blanket of increasingly-sodden mist. Ashmond would
have been having kittens.

Getting this machine from my ex-Chief Pilot had been
surprisingly easy. He'd feigned token resistance at the very
thought of my ever poling one of his machines again but I
knew from Sandra that I was still on company insurance and
that HELIJETS' cashflow was far from healthy. So I'd slapped
all my up-front fifteen hundred over the burn mark on Ashmond's desk, enjoyed watching his senses of vindictiveness
and greed do mental battle and finally got my helicopter.

Just where I was taking that helicopter became known
late on Monday evening with Miss Bird's promised call. Short,

sharp and businesslike as ever, she gave me the co-ordinates for the first pickup. I traced them to the intersecting dotted lines that marked the runways of a disused airfield just inland from the North Norfolk coast. Pickup was by the old control tower and I had to be there at nine a.m.

With the metmen promising the worst I'd left Denbridge early with a full tank of gas. Now even that seventy-five gallons wouldn't be enough for the round trip because reduced speed meant higher consumption per mile. Somewhere along the way I'd have to refuel and that would mean even more flying time and the cost of landing fees. Already fate was making inroads into my profit.

One of the tricks of staying alive in the flying game is being able to sideline future worries. So, with the the GPS clicking off the last decimal miles and the ETA hovering around the desired 0900, I concentrated on the demanding-enough present. I was on the deck now and glued to a twisting country lane that led me groping roughly on track. Beneath my feet, through the chin bubble, I saw what could only be the pot-marked remains of the perimeter track of a disused airfield slide thankfully below. I peered ahead through the murk and saw the ghostly outline of the old control tower, derelict, grey and forlorn, like some aeronautical mausoleum, sitting squat in the middle. I was there.

Dropping the lever, rotor blades slapping, I came banking around it in a tight-banked turn, nose up, speed decelerating, raindrops sluicing off the windshield as, feet to go, I brought the power in again and the increased pitch of the blades cushioned our touchdown on the rubble hardstanding just ten yards from the tower. Back on mother earth, I breathed a sigh of relief and throttled down to ground idle.

Overhead, through the slow-turning blades, the scud swept by. In the rain-drenched tower there was movement. Then they came out. They were a couple but they certainly weren't lovers and more than ever my gut feelings told me I should never have taken this job.

CHAPTER THREE

THEY CAME DUCKING UNDER the blades: two middle-aged sombre men in dark sombre overcoats that were even darker with rain before they were half-way to the machine.

The one leading had a pointed fox-like face and, probably, a body to match beneath the sodden coat. His hair was thin too and blew around like demented straw in the rotor downwash; a man who probably spent lots of money on flashy clothes fighting a losing battle against total shabbiness.

One pace behind and carrying a briefcase was his physical opposite, a gorilla of the type you see hanging around boxing gyms and nightclub doorways: punch-drunk twenty stone collections of muscle and scar tissue with I.Q.s of about the same number. He clambered into the back and his Foxy boss into the front. Pools of rainwater drained onto the cockpit floor and a film of mist formed over the windshield. I nodded to Foxy alongside me and received an equally friendless silent nod in return. No words, just an atmosphere of mutual dislike that suited me just fine.

No spoken words but, from Foxy's pocket, some instructions: a cut-out section of O.S. map with a small area circled in red in the middle of the Fens. It seemed my next landing would be the intersection of a track with one of the huge drainage dykes that cut through this desolately flat reclaimed marshland. A strange location and even stranger further handwritten instructions:

Keep low - don't talk on the radio

Above the smell of sodden clothing came the pervasive stench of latent villainy. I should have shutdown and backed out right there but instead I kept the rotor turning and programmed the co-ordinates into the GPS: forty-seven nautical miles on a heading of 232 degrees. Mercenary instincts were still serving to keep me going, that and a need for excitement in my soul. Miss Bird was right: it took a dumb greedy bastard to pull a number like this whatever it was.

Foxy could have saved himself that note: in this appalling weather, this next leg would be on the deck and no threat to any air traffic. Just aviating us through this meteorological filth would take all of my limited concentration without the distraction of chat on VHF. I slung the card back to Foxy, wound the rotor to 100% and lifted off.

The wonderful birdlike feeling of a helicopter in the hover was something that never failed to give me a kick but I didn't waste too many seconds in revelry that morning. Time and fuel were both short. I pulled pitch and slid the 206 into an accelerating turn that sent us winging away across the disused runways and back into that stinking, precipitating, perfect example of a warm sector depression.

We flew initially dead southwest. That wasn't the heading indicated by the GPS but I knew the direct track would take us straight across the open Wash and in these conditions the last thing I wanted was grey water and no reference. Instead I graunched over the sodden flattening Norfolk farmland, nap-of-the-earthing at seventy knots with me mouthing silent curses and the blower blasting hot air over the slowly clearing windshield.

Winding our meandering course from field to field, the GPS showed our desired track progressively out to starboard. Vague as it was, that south-westerly course took us nicely past the south-east corner of the grey-misted Wash and on into pancake flat Fenland. If you have to scudrun, there's no better place than this and, just a little, I started to relax.

The wind helped too: it had veered westerly and lay pretty well on the nose. Normally, reduced groundspeed was lousy for fuel usage but in this case it meant I could hold a higher, more economic airspeed safely with better control. I eased up the torque to 70% and the speed to eighty; not exactly supersonic but enough to give more miles for the thirty-five gallons of fuel remaining.

Thirty-five gallons: less than an hour and a half and I still had to get to the first drop and then on to some unknown second before I could even think of heading homeward. Somewhere along the way this thirsty bird would definitely need a drink. The GPS was showing a bearing-to-waypoint of 265 degrees and I swung onto it, at the same time picking up the dead-straight dyke whereon lay our mysterious destination.

That extra speed had at least got us to the LZ in fair time with the GPS flicking off its last decimal mile as a roughish track between two rectangular fields came sliding out of the murk at right-angles to our course. At the end was an old five-bar gate and just beyond that, the high embankment of the dyke. I glanced at the still-silent Foxy and he nodded. This was the place.

With fuel ever on my mind, I skipped the recce and brought the 206 straight in, flaring off speed with the nose well up and the blades slapping like a hundred amplified whipcracks. The track itself looked reasonably level and, without even coming to the hover, I just slid the helicopter straight on with the rotor scything the air just yards from the embankment.

Even as the skids touched I heard the rear door open and then the Gorilla was out and vaulting the gate with an agility that would have done credit to the SAS. I'd been wrong thinking he was a boxer; wrestler was more like it. Whatever, he knew where he was going and what he was looking for too and he found them just the other side of that gate.

They were suitcases, two aluminium suitcases of the type that photographers use for their gear. They were glistening with rain but not for much longer because the Gorilla was already heaving them over the gate and following as though all the hounds of hell were on his tail.

Something *was* on his tail alright but it wasn't spectral. Just yards behind the Gorilla, two fit-looking types in blue

berets and combat gear were scrambling up the dyke and aim-
ing Heckler and Koch sub-machine guns right where I didn't
want to be.

'What the....'

'Get going....get airborne!'

They were the first words Foxy had spoken and they came
out almost as a scream but I didn't need any prompting, my
inbuilt survival mode had already clicked in. Even as the Gorilla was slinging the cases into the back I was raising the lever
and lifting off while he was still half-in the door. Above the
scream of engine and gearbox I heard a crack followed almost
instantaneously by a metallic impact in the back end: we were
taking hits. I kicked in some pedal, stuck the nose down the
dyke and zinged us away to the south and safety.

Safety only as long as we were flying. The aircraft seemed
okay but those two Rambos back there had all the appearance
of the long arm of the law and doubtless even now were ra-
dioing my registration letters to H.Q. It wouldn't take long to
have the name of HELIJETS and Tempest to go with them.
There'd be a lot of searching questions before this day was
through and no answers to give.

I forced my mind back to more pressing problems: fuel.
It was down now to twenty and the sooner I knew where we
were going and dropped my load of obnoxious humanity, the
happier I'd be. Beyond that, the less I knew about those cases
and this whole dirty game, the better anyway.

It took a few aimless miles for Foxy to get his act together
and produce another dot on the map that represented some
building just to the south-east of Newmarket. Forty nautical
miles but thankfully close to Cambridge airport and fuel. This
time I didn't even programme the GPS but just rolled into
an approximate heading that would get me into the road and
rail bracket to town. Cloud and rain still raked the treetops
but that wind was with us now and the groundspeed up there.
Even so, I pulled torque to eighty percent and airspeed to a
hundred-and-five and trucked onward.

The flat but not entirely obstructionless Cambridgeshire landscape flashed by. High speed on the deck in quarter-mile visibility is pretty stupid but not half as stupid as landing in some cow pasture and hitching a lift for gas. Twenty-two more nerve-strumming minutes had us at the drop.

I came overhead and made one very quick recce. The buildings turned out to be a house, a large country pseudo-mansion job complete with paddock and stables but, like the two previous drops, totally remote. I dropped the lever and kept the turn going into a descending spiral that had Foxy stiffening in his seat and our skids touching the turf of the horseless paddock in fifteen seconds.

My villainous pair exited, not wasting time or words, Gorilla lugging the two mysterious suitcases to the house, Foxy throwing a nice fat envelope onto the seat beside me. Paid with no thanks and I didn't want any for a dirty job like this; just the relief at seeing him slouch out of my life. Even so, something niggled me, something missing. I couldn't place it and fuel was still my bigger worry. I lifted off and climbed away around the house.

Down below in the driveway, I could see my late pax making for a lime-green Mercedes. It was only a fleeting impression; more important to me was my nine gallon fuel indication. I picked up a heading direct to Cambridge, clicked in their approach frequency and called.

'Cambridge Approach, Helijet five-six-six.'

I gave my flight instead of tail number. The approach controller came straight back.

'Helijet five-six-six, Cambridge approach, go ahead.'

'206 helicopter, seven miles east, low level and requesting straight in for landing.'

'Helijet five-six-six, no conflicting traffic, you're cleared straight in runway two-three. QFE, niner-niner-eight. Call field in sight.'

The fuel gauge was now nudging five gallons, one of which was unusable. With my toes curling over the pedals I stared

ahead for my salvation. Three life-long minutes later I saw
the blessed approach lights and then the runway itself come
sparkling out of the murk.

'Approach, Helijet five-six-six, field in sight.'

'Roger, call tower on one-twenty-two-two.'

I'd got away with it yet again.

SAFE ON THE CAMBRIDGE apron, I shutdown the engine, let the
rotor slow to thirty-percent and then stopped it altogether
with the brake. Peace. After three hours of strumming, my
nerves were ready for a rundown too. I clicked off all the elec-
trics, hung my headset on the hook just below the overhead
panel, climbed out and checked the machine.

There were two clean bullet holes through the fuselage
but well clear of any dynamic components. There'd be questions from Ashmond about that but nothing compared to
questions from others about this whole little jaunt. Well, I'd
tell the truth and trust to my genuine innocence to see me
through. I'd pay my landing fee, get refuelled and then head
straight back to Denbridge to face whatever music awaited
me. I grabbed my envelope of cash and jog-trotted the few
yards through the rain to the terminal building.

A cigarette and coffee were screaming for attention but
first I needed to check-in. In the traffic office, it was warm and
friendly, the front windows looking out over the apron and
the other three walls covered with maps, weather reports and
other general navigation info. This was my world, the world
I knew, loved and missed. To the pretty girl who filled in the
movements book, I gave Newmarket as my point of departure
which was probably pretty common stuff here with all that
horsy set continually coming and going. The landing fee was
thirty-three quid. I tore open my envelope, pulled out a wad
of notes and suddenly felt very very stupid.

In my hand was a wad of useless paper, sheets from a *Yellow
Pages* directory cut to the size of fifty-pound notes. I wanted
to utter one very vulgar heart-felt word but it never came because right then I heard the siren. On an airfield that usually

means an accident but not this time; this wailing, speeding response was coming from town, heading this way and somehow I knew what it was.

Through the traffic office windows, I watched the police car come creaming to a halt right alongside the 206, its siren dying like the last gasp of some demented monster. With it died any hope I'd had of flying back to Denbridge that night. Not moving, I just stood staring as two uniformed officers jumped out and yanked open the helicopter's doors.

The traffic girl glanced nervously in my direction: like me, she knew who they were looking for. I looked down at the wad of *Yellow Pages* in my hand and somehow they symbolised the naivety I'd shown right through this whole crazy show. The police must have told Cambridge to watch for a helicopter before I even reached Newmarket. Air Traffic would have contacted them back the second I called in and confirmed my registration numbers with theirs as soon as I arrived.

Ah well, it only brought the inevitable forward. I looked again at the scene outside: through the rain, the blue light of the police car flashed like a beacon of despair.

It was still flashing when the 206 blew up.

CHAPTER FOUR

AN ARC OF VIVID light, a crack and then the traffic office windows came flying in, a hundred daggers bent on mutilation. We both ducked instinctively but a second later there were hysterical screams from behind the counter. I checked the girl, found nothing more than a few scratches and knew the reaction was all shock.

Out on the apron the police hadn't been so lucky. One now lay a dozen yards from the blazing helicopter, a tangle of lifeless bloody sinews. Close by a second blackened form managed to stagger a few unbelieving steps before collapsing beside the car whose blue light still flashed amongst the flames like some anachronistic Viking funeral ship carrying its crew to the police Valhalla.

Around me crash alarms sounded and people ran but I stood mesmerised, taking in the ramifications of this whole sickly mess. A short while ago I'd been cursing having to break my journey here for fuel; now I realised that heading straight homeward as planned would have seen me and my phoney cash vaporised in an airborne fireball.

There'd been tragic death just the same though. Out there by my blazing machine were two policemen whose colleagues and the law would soon be thirsting for a spot of instant retribution. I stuffed the bundle of pseudo bank notes into my jacket pocket, went back into the terminal entrance and out through the front.

In the carpark, a taxi stood waiting, its driver clambering out to investigate what calamity was enacting airside. I pushed him back in.

'Cambridge.'

'I heard an explosion, mate....a bang.'

'Only some waste fuel being burned off.'

'But I heard the crash alarm?'

'Just a drill.' I climbed into the back. 'Let's get going.'

He wavered for another second, shrugged rounded shoulders, climbed in and started the engine. As we pulled out of the airport we met the city fire service, all lights sirens and speed, coming in. He glanced back suspiciously.

'Must be a big exercise, mate?'

'Yeh, megga. Take me to the city centre.'

'Anywhere in particular?'

The railway station but another hour would see this cabbie being interviewed by Cambridge C.I.D. and the less they knew of my onward movements, the better. Instead I got him to drop me by a department store, walked in the front, out the back and onwards to the station. Ten minutes had me a ticket to London. My mobile phone had gone with the helicopter but I soon found a payphone and dialled *HELIJETS*.

'Mike; not calling to stand me up again are you?'

It was good to hear Sandra's voice on the other end and even better to realise the police hadn't touched base yet.

'No, but there's been a small change of plan. I'll need you to meet me at Barking tube station late this evening.'

It didn't take a psychiatrist to suss the strain in my voice. 'What's wrong, Mike? Why aren't you flying back? Is there a snag with the helicopter?'

'Yeah, a big one.' I took a deep breath. 'Look, Sandra, very shortly someone's going to call Ashmond to tell him his precious helicopter has just been reduced to sixteen hundred pounds of aluminium scrap. Shortly after that the police are going to be seriously descending and it'll be me they're wanting. You haven't heard from me, understand.'

'I....I think so.' This was a bit out of her league. 'Mike, what's happening? Are you all right? Do you want me to bring your car or mine?'

In my pocket were the keys to my house and car.

'Yours, Sandra. Better anyway so you don't look too involved.'

'Involved in what for goodness sake? Mike, can't you tell me anything?'

'Later; my train's in. I'll call you from Liverpool Street with an E.T.A. for Barking.'

I hung up and ran. It was one of those railcar jobs, open plan and horribly public but the smoking compartment in these health-kick days was reasonably sparse. I lit up, watched the environs of Cambridge draw fast astern, relaxed a bit and tried to work out what had happened to my world.

Not hard, I'd been suckered into providing fail-safe transportation for some evil heist, the centre point of which had been those aluminium cases. Whatever they contained, the police were on to it, had somehow known there was going to be a collection and laid on their own little sting. Very nearly succeeded too. With the goods left in such a remote area they'd been expecting a car or motorbike or even a speedboat down the dyke. What they hadn't allowed for was a helicopter and some pilot dumb enough to fly it.

The only snag in this clever plan had been my being able to identify the villains later. That was one problem easily disposed off. I knew now what had been bugging me at Newmarket, what had been missing: the briefcase the Gorilla had been carrying when they boarded. He'd probably been setting the timer even as we landed but they hadn't allowed for me needing fuel. I looked out of the train windows at the scud still flying by overhead and thanked my stars it had slowed me so much this morning.

The train stopped at the dozen or so stations between Cambridge and London and every passenger that got on looked remarkably like plainclothes police. Stressful as all this was, I still didn't regret skipping the scene. In the eyes of many this would only cement my guilt but to me it was a case of no surrender. With freedom I had time and with time there was hope. Hope for what? I was still struggling with that one when we pulled into Liverpool Street.

• • •

'Mike, are you okay? I've been worried sick.'

Sandra was waiting outside the tube station in her blue mini when I emerged into the darkness. I climbed in beside her.

'Just about; what's been happening at your end?'

She grimaced.

'Just like you said, all hell broke loose. First of all Cambridge called and broke the news to Captain Ashmond. Thanks to your warning I had a cup of strong black coffee already brewed. Half an hour later the police arrived, uniformed and C.I.D. They spent a long time with Captain Ashmond but they were obviously looking for you.'

'How did he take it?'

She rolled big blue eyes.

'Badly; insurance should take care of the helicopter but it's all the bad publicity that will really hurt. The five-o-clock news said that two policemen had been killed,' she glanced towards me sadly, 'Mike, how could you get involved with something like that?'

'I'll explain it all later, Sandra; right now let's go to the flat so I can collect some gear.'

'Is that safe?'

'I won't know until we get there; let's hurry.'

We drove off amongst the rest of the evening homegoers, ordinary people living ordinary lives heading towards ordinary homes; I'd never been one of them and probably never would be now. While Sandra crawled with the rest I gave her the full story from Miss Bird onwards. She listened with mounting disapproval.

'You should have stayed and talked to the police, Mike. If you've done nothing wrong you had nothing to fear.'

'I wouldn't bet on it. Before I go pleading innocence I'm going to have Miss Bird - or whatever her real name is - right there alongside me to prove it.' I wound down the window and lit another cigarette. 'Any idea who this girl is?'

She shook her head.

'Not from the name or your description but I only take

bookings by phone, fax or E-mail and hardly ever meet the charter agent personally.' Her smile back to me was down-turned with regret. 'Sorry I can't be of more help, Mike.'

I tousled her cropped blonde thatch.

'You're all the help in the world just being here, Sandra.' We were in my street now but there was one big difference to when I'd left it twelve hours previous: a police car right there in my own parking slot. I slunk down in my seat. 'Keep going; don't even slow or look.'

Across the street was a little knot of sightseers; I stayed well down until we'd turned the corner at the other end. San-dra took a deep breath.

'No kit for you, Captain Tempest.' She paused long enough to give an impish grin. 'I guess you'll have to slum it and share my toothbrush tonight.'

I'd had worse offers but now wasn't the time to be using people, especially a good friend like Sandra.

'Harbouring a fugitive of the law? Could get you into trouble.'

She laughed.

'As long as you don't.'

My local Asian newsagents went sliding by with the eve-ning addition placarded outside.

LADY TRACAM KIDNAP
HELICOPTER GANG SOUGHT

We stopped and Sandra bought a paper.

'So, it's kidnapping you're involved in?'

Sandra was questioning me over the top of her coffee mug and even the cosiness of her first-floor pad didn't allay the chill of her words.

'Unwittingly, yes.' I emptied my own mug, laid down the paper and flashed up another cig. 'The only crumb of com-fort I can find in all this mess is that the old girl may still be handed back alive.'

'But not even kidnapped when you agreed to do the job in the first place.'

I winced at that fact gleaned from the paper.

'No; she left her sports club in Henley at eleven a.m. last Sunday and wasn't heard of again until her husband received the ransom demand for six million quid.'

'Pricey woman.' Sandra got up and fetched an ashtray before lighting the cigarette I'd just tossed her. 'Who is she anyway, this Lady Tracam?'

'Wife of Sir John Tracam, aging millionaire entrepreneur and philanthropist. He was at some religious retreat in Scotland when they snatched her. The demand was phoned into his London corporate headquarters the same day. Staff got in touch with him and he flew straight down and contacted Scotland Yard.' I threw the newspaper across so she could see the photo of the couple taken at one of their charity dinners. They were in evening dress, she a handsome middle age, he a tall grey-haired white-bearded octogenarian with an athletic leanness that looked three decades less.

Sandra glanced at it sadly.

'He took a chance, didn't he, going to the police when they'd warned him not to?'

I shook my head.

'Not statistically; the British police have had an almost total recovery in kidnap cases since the McKaye fiasco. They simply followed their standard procedure of imposing a total news blackout and setting their trap at the kidnapper's most vulnerable point: the ransom collection. This time, though, it didn't work.'

'Thanks to we-know-who.'

Once again, I flinched slightly.

'Yeh, and so do they.' I pulled the paper back and read from it:

"The police are anxious to interview pilot Michael Tempest who, they believe, flew the helicopter used in the ransom pickup."

Sandra sat in thought for a few seconds and then stubbed her half-smoked cigarette.

'Mike, you've got to give yourself up to the police. Surely your helicopter being sabotaged and you obviously the target is clear enough proof that you were just caught up in a plan you knew nothing about?'

'Not necessarily; the police might just as easily conclude I was one of the gang and the rest just wanted to cut me out of the shareout. Honour-amongst-thieves is a concept about as mythical as my thousand quid payoff.' I threw my wad of cut *Yellow Pages* onto the coffee table where they went scattering like my dreams of quick-earned dosh.

It was Sandra's turn to shake her head.

'Running off like that only made you look more guilty and the longer you run, Mike, the worse it will look. Why don't you just tell the police all you know and let them do the finding?'

Now wasn't time to explain my inherent aversion to capture but perhaps this time the other side were my side after all. I took hold of her hand.

'Okay, lets see what the evening news has to say and then perhaps we'll call the police.'.

'Good.' She switched on the box with the air of someone making a breakthrough in common sense.

The Tracam kidnap was the main item. It showed local film of the pickup site then the burntout wreckage of my 206 and the police car. Even some interviews at the big house and stables where I'd made my last drop. No clues there; it was empty and for sale as explained by locals who'd seen me come in and out. But I watched all this through a haze of anguish because the news had started with the worst revelation of all: in just the last hour Lady Tracam's body had been discovered on the North Norfolk coast. She'd been strangled.

'Ugh, poor woman." I felt Sandra's hand tighten in mine but, minutes later, it was mine tightening in hers as I watched the end of the extended programme. It was a police news conference and had a distraught Sir John making a heartfelt plea for help leading to the arrest of his wife's murderers. He was backing it up with a reward of hard cash too: two hundred and fifty thousand pounds.

I told Sandra my plan and that night slept fitfully and alone on the couch.

'YOU'RE CRAZY!' SANDRA WAS never one to mince words and breakfast next morning was pure recrimination. 'So now, instead of going to the police and getting things sorted, you plan on wasting time and effort, not to mention further deepening your own involvement, by pratting around on some futile Sherlock Holmes kick to find the culprits yourself. I always knew you were mental but this confirms it.'

With encouragement like that I couldn't go wrong.

'Look, Sandra, this is probably the last chance I'll ever get to make myself some real cash. I know things about this case that the police don't but, as yet, I can't give them names. Don't forget that gang will still want me dead and if I can get to them first and make a quarter-million at the same time, what's wrong with that?'

She stubbed her cigarette with feeling.

'Everything. A fat lot of good revenge and a few thousand quid are going to do you in gaol. And what do you have really? A description of two crooks and their car. What do you propose doing with that? Walk around London looking for them?'

I lit my fourth that morning.

'You're forgetting Miss Bird. Find her and I reckon she'll lead me to the rest of the rotten crew.'

'Find her. How? Put an ad in the local paper?'

I ignored the sarcasm.

'No, I'm going to take a run down to Battersea and see Helen. I reckon if anyone knows our Miss Bird it'll be her.'

Helen Winters did passenger handling at Battersea Heliport. Sandra knew her over the phone.

'You used to go out with her didn't you? She'll probably turn you in out of sheer spite. Why not just call her.'

'No she won't, Helen's not like that, but the phone's no good. This needs the personal touch.'

She didn't seem convinced.

'How will you get there?'

I shrugged.

'Tube and bus, I guess.'

She grabbed her keys off the sideboard and tossed them across.

'You'd better take my mini; the less public sleuths that spot your ugly face, the better. I'll ring in sick. I don't think I could face Captain Ashmond this morning anyway.'

I put them in my pocket and gave her a heartfelt kiss.

'Thanks, Sandra. When I've got that reward I'll make it all up.'

She gave a scoffing laugh, scooped up the phoney payoff still scattered over the coffee table from the night before and threw it across.

'Well try and get *real* money this time.'

I looked down at the cutup *Yellow Pages* and noticed something I hadn't seen before: a small display ad in the original directory that someone had heavily circled.

SMALLBRIGHT'S TRAVELLING FUNFAIR

Below the heading were details of its various rides and attractions and a number to call. Why had someone marked this? Probably because they were simply looking for an evening's entertainment. I stuffed it into my pocket anyway, binned the rest and grabbed my flight jacket off the chairback.

'Time to go.'

She saw me to the door.

'Take care....and....and, Mike....'

I paused squeezing into the mini.

'Yeh?'

'You don't have to make a fortune for me; I'll settle for an overdraft anytime.'

I blew her a kiss and slammed the door. If I didn't get hustling and find Miss Bird and her boys it would be the Bank of Luck and Life that would be giving me the red-ink treatment and overdrafts there tended to be painful and permanent.

I revved the mini and headed citywards.

CHAPTER FIVE

WITH DRIZZLE DESCENDING STEADILY and mistily onto the Victorian edifices of the south bank, London that morning pretty well mirrored my mood. Beyond the thumping wipers, vehicles and buildings alike pitted their miserable wattage against the all-pervading stygian gloom while the few brave souls scuttling the rain-blackened streets resembled some misplaced Lowry painting brought horribly to miserable life.

A quick stop at a newsagent enroute didn't help. Not only was the Tracam kidnapping still making the front pages but some of the morning editions now had my mug-shot straight from the Civil Aviation files. It was a few years old and didn't do a thing for my ego but it did make me beat a hasty retreat back to the car feeling that the eyes of the world were now upon me. I set off down York Road, keeping a wary eye for roving police cars and realising more than ever the desperate loneliness of a man on the run. Half a mile short of the heliport I spotted a payphone and pulled in.

'Helen....Mike Tempest.'

'My God, Mike...,' a classy girl, Helen, with an accent to match, '...where are you? Is it true what the papers are saying?'

'Probably, but not the way you think. I need to talk to you, Helen. If I come to the heliport can you meet me in the carpark....discreetly?'

There was a small sigh and a pause and then, 'All right; give me fifteen minutes?'

A second's apprehension.

'Okay, but I'm trusting you, Helen. No calls to the police; I need your help.'

'I promise, Mike,' she sounded a bit hurt, 'but I'll want the truth.'

'You'll get it.'

I hung up and wheeled off the last half mile before turning right between the disused warehouses and run-down offices that lined the narrow approach road. No room here to do a one-eighty if the law were waiting at the other end but the carpark, when I reached it, produced no surprises. I parked by the apron fence, lit a cigarette and took in my old stomping ground.

There was the usual early-morning gaggle of miscellaneous helicopters on the rain-slick apron: a couple of Jet Rangers, a corporate A-Star and a smart all-black twin-engine Bolkow 105 that I'd never seen before. No pilots in sight but I probably knew most of them and could guess what they were doing now: slurping coffee together in the small terminal and discussing how Mike Tempest had finally dropped his dumb ass right in it.

After ten minutes they started to emerge with their pax and one by one turbines fired, rotors turned and helicopters hover-taxied to the stub runway and transitioned over the Thames. Life in the aviation world seemed to be carrying on distressingly smoothly without me. Soon the ramp held only the all-black Bolkow and the scent of burnt Avtur that came drifting back like incense off the altar of my professional sacrifice.

A tap on my side window startled me out of my musings but it was Helen bearing two plastic cups of steaming coffee. I wound the window, took the cups and let her in the other side.

'Helen, you're an angel; you've saved my life.'

'Well, it seems you're not making a very good job of it yourself.' She took her cup between long manicured fingers, flicked back straight fair hair and crossed shapely legs. 'You seem to have got yourself in a real mess this time, Mike; the reports are awful.'

'I'm innocent, Helen....honest.'

'Tell me about it then....and the truth.'

I did, missing nothing. Well, almost nothing; I didn't say

anything about going after the reward because a woman was bound to misunderstand that sort of thing but I did give her a full description of the elusive Miss Bird plus all my theories and suspicions.

'I need to find this girl, Helen. Ring any bells?'

She lit a cigarette, handed it to me and then lit another for herself before sitting for a minute the way classy birds do: cigarette and cig-arm vertical with the elbow cupped in the other hand.

'She sounds awfully like a girl I've seen here once or twice meeting helicopters. Runs her own charter agency, I think. Never talked very much.'

Hope shone eternal.

'That sounds just like her. A name, Helen....have you got her real name?'

Helen closed her eyes and ran a hand through her hair. If the exercise was meant to stir the brain cells it failed.

'Mike, I can't remember.' She sounded genuinely upset.

'Well try for goodness sakes; this is really important.' I softened my tone when I saw I was only making things worse. 'How about her company name; perhaps you can remember that?'

The poor girl reclosed fast-watering eyes and held a worried brow in mock meditation.

'I can see her now, wearing that fawn trenchcoat you described and some sort of identification badge with the company and her own name,' she gave an extra squeeze of the eyes for good measure, 'Death....something like that.'

'You're joking; her name's Death? You mean Death pronounced Dee-ath.'

She shook her head.

'No, Death or Dying or something like that and she had a funny Christian name too.' Helen was trying hard but pressure was only driving the memory further away and she finally dropped her hand in exasperation. 'Mike, I'm sorry; it's gone completely.'

'Don't worry, you've helped a lot.' I said it with more

chivalry than feeling but if I changed the subject perhaps the recall would click back. I nodded towards the solitary all-black Bolkow still standing on the apron; something I wouldn't mind poling one day if I could just keep my licence out of the Civil Aviation shredder. 'Nice machine; who owns it, Helen?'

She was relieved to be finally asked something answerable.

'It belongs to some offshore operating company called OCEANIC GEOPHYSICAL except they spell Oceanic funny,' she gave it to me letter by letter, 'O-S-S-I-A-N-I-C.... OSSIANIC GEOPHYSICAL. The 105 flew in here a couple of days ago off one of their survey ships....the MORRIGAN. The pilot's an American with one of those Irish-sounding names....begins with an O....' she closed her eyes again, this time with more success, '....Kane; that's right, O-Kane. Hard-looking type.' She stubbed her cigarette, took my empty cup, stuck it inside her own and gave me a quick peck on the cheek. 'Must go now, Mike; lots to do. Sorry I can't be of more help. Where can I reach you if I remember that name?....Mike'

I was miles away.

'Oh....yeh....thanks, Helen. I'll give you a call in a day or so.'

She gave me a questioning look and departed, probably wondering why she gave me the time of day anyway. The wind was getting up now, kicking the sock on the orange and white pole. I lit another cigarette off the old butt and tried to sort some order into the thoughts tumbling around my tired brain. People with names I'd wanted to lose. People without names I wanted to find. Time to forget the former and do some more about the latter. I started the engine and was about to pull out when the taxi arrived and two people got out.

I didn't know her. She was reasonably good looking in a brazen sort of way: a peroxide blonde, tall and slim-figured under leopard-skin coat pulled tight about her.

I knew him though. I'd thought him long-time dead but here he was very much alive and not much changed in spite of all he'd been through. Perhaps the close-cropped hair was greyer now but the pockmarked face still looked like a lunar landscape broken only by the vivid scar that ran from left ear to cruel mouth. I couldn't see his eyes because they were hidden by tinted lenses in steel aviator frames but I could imagine them as icily cold as ever. Perhaps the muscular frame was stooped a little now but even under the flight jacket it still generated menace and a sense of latent aggression.

I thought at first they were lovers and then decided just as quickly there was anything but love between these two. He paid off the cab and strode straight out to the Bolkow leaving her to struggle behind with heavy cases and high heels. By the time she reached the helicopter he was in and already winding the turbines. He let her get the cases into the back and her into the front but only just and then he was pulling pitch and getting light on the skids.

No external checks; no cockpit checks. He still flew in the old kick-the-tyres-light-the-fires way he had and as he was still alive and still flying, I guessed it hadn't served him that badly anyway. Always a bad airman but still a good pilot: that stocky two tonnes of technology didn't even twitch as he lifted her smoothly off, cleared the ramp and accelerated into a climbing turn straight into the enveloping overcast.

I departed too, not so dramatically and, hopefully, not so easily recognised. With wipers still thumping, I picked my way back east. Rain still fell, lights still burned, people still scurried but I was somewhere else in a country half a world away where beautiful tropical dawns were broken by the rattle of machine gun fire, the days filled with death and the cries of stricken innocents and the blood-red glow of sunset clouded by black smoke rising from whichever village that day had known the futile cost of civil war.

And he'd loved every minute of it.

I should have asked Helen where the Bolkow was headed. Not that it mattered anyway because wherever it was, the distance wouldn't be far enough between me and Killer O-Kane.

THAT WAS THE OLD past; the immediate past was bad enough
and the immediate future very much dependent on how I
handled the present. I pulled into the next greasepit cafe that
appeared on the left.

I was taking a chance but it met my basic requirements:
few punters, bucket-sized mugs of coffee, a payphone and a
proprietor good on lending his directories and, hopefully, bad
on faces. I picked a secluded table behind the fruit machine,
lit a cigarette and looked up the Deaths. There turned out to
be more than in the *Times* obituary column and that's where
I'd be myself by the time I'd rung them all. I turned instead to
the *Yellow Pages* and looked up *Charter Agencies*.

There were plenty of those too but here at least I could
do some pruning. For starters, I doubted that she had her own
aircraft so out went all the air taxi operators. Unlikely also
that her business was a large one so I scratched all the big
outfits with display ads. Of course, she could be an employee
but I had to start somewhere and besides, something told me
Miss Bird was very much her own boss. Even so, the cut-down
list was still ten entries long and I sipped my coffee trying to
think of some other eliminating factor.

Was there anything she'd said that cold morning under
Tower Bridge that would give me some clue? Tower Bridge;
why did she choose that as a venue anyway? Close to her office perhaps? Doubtful; rental rates around there were bigger
than the phone numbers. Not an easy place to park a car either so how did she get there? There were plenty of options:
cab, tube trains, buses, light railway, even Thames river boats.
I doubted if the latter had much appeal to the fast-moving
Ms Death and the first three could apply to any location in
London. That left just the light railway.

The more I thought about it, the more that fast transit
system seemed a possibility: Docklands and its high tech com-
mercial image would be definitely the scene for Miss Bird.
Following this hunch, I went for only those entries having
an *E* area postcode. There were only three. I fished out some
change and went to the payphone.

I should have used one outside but in here was a good twenty degrees warmer and there was only one other punter anyway, a flat-capped character munching his bacon butty two tables away. I punched off the first number of ALL TRANS-PORT.

The girl who answered was very polite, very young and very sure that no Miss Death or Dee-ath worked or had ever worked in her small office. In fact, she explained sweetly, there were only two girls at ALL TRANSPORT and they were both under twenty-one. Nice for them but a complete wipe-out for thirty-three percent of my prospects. I was about to invest another ten pence of my savings when I glanced back to Flatcap on the far table.

He was enjoying his mug of tea now together with the sporting page of his favourite tabloid. Nothing wrong with that except the front page facing me had 250,000 POUNDS REWARD and my photo plastered right across. I should have got out there and then but success might be just one call away and he seemed a long way yet from abandoning the sports page. I dialled the second number.

It wasn't even a female who answered at COURTESY TRAVEL and if the pompous bigot who did was the owner, then naming his company must have been the only spark of humour he'd ever had. No, he most certainly had no girl working for him and no time either to answer fatuous ques-tions. No more customers either with luck but he was now the least of my worries: at the far table the butty gourmet had left the sporting world and was working his way, Chinese fashion, backwards to the front. Judging by his scant reading of the innards, it wouldn't take him long to get there either. I des-perately banged in my last ten p. and clicked off the number for EXECUTIVE EXPRESS.

By the third ring, Matey had reached the front page. Come on, answer, damn you. Now he was looking at my pic-ture, then at me and then back to the picture. By the time the other end answered I knew he'd recognised me.

CHAPTER SIX

THERE WAS THE SQUEAK of one of those infernal answering machines and then a female voice thanking me for calling EX-ECUTIVE EXPRESS and assuring her prompt attention if I left my name and number.

I left neither and put the phone down; I'd found Miss Bird. Unfortunately, Flatcap in the corner had found me. While he wavered on what was probably the biggest decision of his life, I made a mental note of her address - 336 Windjammer Court, Benbow Street, E14 - and headed for the door.

He stood up uncertainly, the thought of making a fool of himself just enough to stay his hand. I headed for the mini and flashed away but not without catching a final glimpse of Flatcap dialling three numbers on the payphone and watching me go.

Not good; now the law would have a description of my car and an area to concentrate their search. Dumping Sandra's mini would have made the most sense but time now was vital: Miss Bird would know I was still inconveniently alive and silent messages coming through the answering machine might scare her away for good. On the other hand, she might invite nasty friends around for tea, neither option being much use to me. I sped eastwards through the rain for Tower Bridge, the north bank and Docklands.

THE ISLE OF DOGS. Not the loveliest of names and not even an island really, just a U-shaped spit of inner city formed by a sharp meander of the River Thames with the old West India Docks completing its southern "shore". In the old days its image had been one of darkened warehouses, shadowy wharves and sinister backstreets but the ships were long gone now and in their place rose corporate headquarter and luxury penthouse. This was the "business city for the twenty-first century", as all the glossy brochures proclaimed it.

But Benbow Street, when I found it, was still very much in the twentieth. I pulled in by the curb looking up at Windjammer Court. It was very different to what I'd imagined. Six storeys high, red-bricked and ugly, a block of council flats built in the late fifties on ground cleared a decade earlier by the Luftwaffe. Did EXECUTIVE EXPRESS really operate from here? I stubbed my cigarette, spun the mini into the walled parking area and set off to find out.

Close up, the building improved: many of the ground floor units, presumably now privately owned, had been transformed by replacement leaded windows, boxed conifers and hanging baskets. The upper levels hadn't received the same treatment though they did enjoy one advantage over the ground: balconies with french windows leading into their lounges. The main doors at the front led only to the ground floor flats; 336 would be on the third. Collar up against the sleeting wind, I walked round to the rear.

Back there, the outside doors were of the same heavy wood but decidedly less cared for: peeling varnish, blackening bare patches, the incipient rot of neglect and none of my concern. Ten yards away was something that was.

Parked opposite the doors was a lime-green Mercedes. A few days ago, one just like it should have been the last car I ever saw. This one had a personalised registration: STF 1. Why were those letters vaguely familiar? I couldn't think but I knew the enemy were here. I went inside.

In the hallway the decor was stark bare concrete and the atmosphere rancid with the smell of stale urine. To the left was a battered lift with the doors closed and indicator showing second floor. I let it stay there and went up the stairs; harder on my pulse rate but better than getting it stopped altogether not knowing who was waiting at the other end.

I climbed upwards with only the vaguest notion of strategy; knocking on the door didn't seem too smart anymore. A good listen outside might be the best immediate plan; if the whole gang were here, a quick call to Tracam's corporate HQ and Scotland Yard would get things moving. Passing the second floor, I noticed the lift doors closing.

The indicator lights flickered upwards. They didn't flicker far; even before I reached the third I heard them opening and closing at that level and when I got there the landing was empty. Then the indicator lights blinked down to the ground floor.

I needed to know who'd taken that lift. At each floor level there was a waist-high open parapet overlooking front and rear carparks. I stood to the side of the rear one, back to the wall in best private-eye manner. The lift thumped bottom and the groundfloor doors opened. I was about thirty-five feet up but there was no mistaking the two figures in dark overcoats scuttling towards the lime-green Merc. They didn't exactly spin wheels driving out but Foxy and Gorilla were certainly in a hurry.

I was in a hurry too, to get this whole nasty business wrapped up and behind me; I'd lost two of them but at least the one remaining made for easier handling. I went through to the inner hall.

The heavy fire-door self-closed behind me. Poor lighting and bare brickwork here and the renderings of some local rock station that got ever louder as I neared flat 336.

I stood outside Miss Bird's front door. It was a smart one; the others were all cheap flush jobs whereas hers was panelled white gloss with solid brass furniture. In the centre was a card-holder containing an EXECUTIVE EXPRESS business card. Amongst all the other data was a name:

Crestovana Dysart
Proprietor

Dysart, pronounced DIE-sart. Helen's Deathly recollection hadn't been totally off the beam and Crestovana was unusual enough to set it apart from all the Sharons and Traceys.

With a name like that I would have expected better taste
in music; the front door was almost vibrating to the reverbera-
tions of heavy-metal rock. I went to finger the brass bellpush,
saw the fisheye security lens in the middle of the door and
thought better of it: small chance of her opening without seeing a face on the other side and even less if she did. Instead I
settled for a quick recce through the letter-box.

I could see nothing but empty inner hall while the beat
of that hideous music abused my ears. Another of my senses
was reacting too: from out of flat 336 came the unmistakable
reek of supremely efficient, non-toxic but lethally explosive
natural North Sea gas.

I pulled back and tried the door: locked. I banged hard on
the brass knocker: no response. No ringing of bells now; one
spark and Windjammer Court would be doing its own version
of Krakatoa. Batter down the door? I dismissed the idea even
as I thought it; this whole building would be collapsing around
it before I knocked down that hunk of hardwood. Only one
other way; I went to the neighbour's door and knocked.

No reply which was a pity because I needed their balcony
and quick because any minute now someone would be making a spark-buzzing call on Crestovana Dysart's phone and I
could guess just who. I went to the next and last flat on this
side: no-one there either. Only one thing for it; I went back
out through the firedoors and looked over the parapet. There
was a narrow ridge of brickwork running level with the base
of the balconies. It was about four inches wide and it bridged
the three gaps of the two balconies between here and Miss
Dysart's. Was it structural or ornamental? One way to find
out: I climbed over the parapet and planted my trainers on
the ledge.

So far, so good with the parapet still there to hang on to;
the real test would be the next fifteen feet where there was
nothing. I set off, hands flat to the brickwork, shuffling along
like some rock-climbing penguin, thankful that this face of
Windjammer Court was at least in the lee of the bitter north-
east wind and rain.

It was slow progress and each shuffle took a year off my life. Everyone thinks that pilots must have a carefree disregard of heights. How wrong they are; it's all a matter of perspective and those three storeys of vertical wall down to the hard ground gave me all the perspective I could have done without.

Finally, after much gritting of teeth and tearing of nails, I made the first balcony. I climbed over its parapet but paused only briefly amid deck chairs and potted conifers before pushing on again across the next gap.

Why was I doing this? Certainly not for any moral reasons. Still in my mind was the lure of that reward and for that I needed a talking Crestovana, not a dead Dysart. Simple as that. At least it kept my mind off the immediate predicament and got me to the next balcony, fingers bloodied but mentally unbowed. This time I didn't pause at all but pushed straight on for the third and final ledge, checking as I did so if I had any spectators to my bad imitation of Spiderman. I hadn't, the rain was keeping the streets pretty clear, but what did discourage me at this level were the french windows.

They were metal framed with small panes that Houdini himself couldn't have squeezed through. How would I? One problem at a time, Tempest. I shuffled on, the encouraging sound of muffled rock creeping closer and me going faster as I got the hang of this brick-walking act.

With over-confidence setting in, the result was almost inevitable: two feet from the balcony of 336 I slipped.

CHAPTER SEVEN

As ONE FOOT WENT I pushed off with the other and flung myself over the balcony parapet. A gap of two more inches would have raspberry-jammed me into the carpark; instead I ended up with my arms crocked over the coping and my legs flailing below like some demented string-puppet with St Vitas dance.

With strength going and my wits nigh on gone I used what remained of both to heave myself up, get one hand on top, push downwards and bring my chest up onto the coping. A good push with my other hand and I was over, sprawled in the quarry-tiled well of the balcony with my feet tangled in the wrought-iron back of a patio chair. It was about as undignified a re-entrance back into Crestovana Dysart's life as I could manage, assuming she still had one left to be undignified in.

I'd soon know; I pulled myself to my feet and looked through the small-paned french windows at a cosily furnished lounge still pulsating to the beat of heavy rock but otherwise devoid of life, In the lock on the other side was a key. I picked up a patio chair, put its metal leg through the pane nearest the lock and followed with my hand. Two seconds and I was in.

The stench of gas hit me like a boxer's left hook. Natural gas isn't poisonous but it'll never get bottled by Dior either. Holding my breath, I stumbled on into the open-plan kitchen and one by one slapped off the hissing cooker taps. Getting to them hadn't been a straight run: I'd had to step over the body of a woman enroute.

She was sprawled before the oven, a slim figure almost childlike in jeans and tee shirt, face expressionless but familiar: Crestovana Dysart. I went back to the french windows,

threw them wide open, breathed a lungful of fresh air and
went back in.

The stereo still blared its cacophony; so tempting to
switch it off but I was scared to switch anything until the gas
had cleared completely. I settled for turning the volume right
down, went back to the kitchen and picked up Miss Dysart.

She was blessedly light and thankfully still warm as I carried her out onto the balcony and laid her on the tiles in ice-
cold air that would have revived Tutankhamen. I knelt down
beside her, saw just the smallest rise and fall of the white tee-
shirt and knew Old Nick had missed out again. Soon she was
twitching arms and legs with her head rolling from side to
side.

I went back into the lounge and found the gas had almost
cleared. Opposite the kitchen was a computer and printer and
next to that a filing cabinet with telephone and answering
machine on top. This was the office of EXECUTIVE EX-
PRESS. Even as I looked at it, the phone rang.

I'd been expecting this call but even with the gas seemingly gone those three rings seemed like the death knell. I
lifted the receiver and just as quickly replaced it hoping it
would sound like the sudden disconnect of flat 336 erupting
in a gas-fuelled fireball.

Miss Dysart needed fire but not that sort. There were
drinks on the sideboard on the other side of the room. I
poured a good half tumblerfull of brandy, went out and held
it under her nose. Just the fumes were enough to get those
long-lashed lids flickering and then opening. I pulled her into
a sitting position and tried to get some Napoleon down her
throat. A lot spilled from the corner of her mouth but some
hit the mark because she gave a sudden cough and shivered in
my arms. Glazed bewildered eyes met mine followed by slow
comprehension and speech.

'You.'

'Me.' A flurry of wind licked the balcony and ruffled her
hair. Beneath the thin cotton tee-shirt she gave an involun-
tary tremble. 'Let's get you inside.'

I helped her into an armchair, went to the bedroom, pulled off the flowered duvet and wrapped it round her. Sitting there cocooned, hands cupping the brandy tumbler, she looked a pathetically vulnerable shadow of the self-assured businesswoman I'd met at Tower Bridge. Her voice was still shaky and barely audible.

'How did you find me?'

'Not easily,' I closed the french windows, came back and leaned against the kitchen counter, 'but a man can do most things when its a case of that or life in prison.'

Long slender fingers tightened around the tumbler.

'I'm so sorry....,' with the faltering speech came tears. They looked pretty genuine to me. If they weren't, she'd missed her place at RADA,'....I never knew....that poor woman....murdered....and I helped.'

That was a story I looked forward to hearing later. Right now there were other questions. I glanced around the room.

'What happened here?'

She bit her lip, pirouetting on the edge of hysteria.

'Those two men....came here....turned up the radio....held something over my mouth....chloroform I think.'

A pretty generous dose to keep her under that long but they weren't taking too big a risk; if she'd come round and switched off the radio she'd have just saved them, a phone call. I stood up.

'Are you ready to travel?'

'Travel?' She was confused and after her experience I couldn't blame her but I wasn't going to go easy just yet.

'Yes, travel. You can't stay here. Your lovely friends will only have to scan the evening rags to see that Windjammer Court hasn't relocated into the Thames and then they'll be back to do a better job.' I let that sink in. 'The sooner we're both out of here, the better.'

'I see,' she ran fingers through her hair, 'I suppose you're going to hand me in to the police.' There was colour coming back into her face but it was still a picture of confusion mixed with a little despair as she added, 'I wouldn't blame you.'

'Not until I've heard your story.' I took the empty tumbler from her hand and put it on the counter. 'How are you feeling now?'

She grimaced.

'Splitting headache but nothing an aspirin won't put right.' In spite of the tears, this was some tough little cookie and there was sincerity in her voice when she said, 'and thanks, Mike....for everything....it's more than I deserve.'

She was right there but a bit of compassion wouldn't go amiss.

'Miss Dysart, I don't think either of us deserved the agro this little number's brought us.' Time to sort out more immediate problems before they came to sort out us. 'Do you have a car?'

'Yes, a jeep in the carpark below.'

I took the duvet from her shoulders.

'Right, you go pack a bag; the main thing now is to put some miles behind us.'

The smile was fleeting but an improvement nonetheless.

'Okay.'

I helped her up and into the bedroom. She wouldn't be running the ten thousand metres just yet but at least she was maintaining the vertical. I left her stuffing clothes into a large canvas grip, went to light a cigarette and then reckoned this flat had had enough noxious fumes for one day. Instead I made a quick call on her phone and then taped a bin liner over the smashed pane. It would do for now.

I glanced again round her little pad: neat, clean and homely. On top of the sideboard was the framed photo of a young boy in school uniform. When she came out she slipped it into the canvas grip, smiled and said, 'Ready.'

'What about EXECUTIVE EXPRESS?' I cocked my head towards her desk.

She smiled again and slipped on a quilted anorak.

'Half an hour ago I was almost out of business for good. I rather think EXECUTIVE EXPRESS can go to hell for a few days.'

I rather thought so too as I heaved the bag over my shoulder and followed its owner down the stairs and out to the little blue jeep. We didn't say anything. Perhaps we both guessed that things would get a lot worse before they got better.

WE HEADED FOR NORTH London, me driving, the rain playing its own drum solo on the canvas top. I kept the speed down and my attention on the girl talking beside me.

'I think I owe you some explanations, Mike.'

'I think you do, *Miss Bird.*' I deliberately emphasised the alias and the little laugh she gave in return broke the ice.

'Yes, I'm sorry about the *non de plume*. My name's Crestovana Dysart as you probably now know but I'm called Cress for short.'

'Okay....Cress....from the beginning.'

'All right. Well, I started EXECUTIVE EXPRESS about five years ago. I was working for a charter company, saw a need for an air taxi agency, hired myself some office equipment and was in business.' I nodded, trying to show I'd pretty well worked all that out for myself so she went on, 'Things were quite profitable until recently but this downturn in the market hit me hard. Bills were piling up, the mortgage on the flat, school fees....I've got a young son.'

'The boy in the photo?'

'Yes, Robin, he's twelve and at boarding school. Anyway, things were getting pretty desperate and then that horrid little man called me.'

'Foxy?'

'Foxy,' she smiled, 'is that what you call him? What a good name; yes, him. He said he was calling in response to an ad I'd been running, said he had this job he wanted to discuss with me.'

Four p.m. Lights were on now though most of them had probably never been off. Already, some early leavers were splashing homeward to slippers and telly. I flashed up a cigarette from the dashboard lighter.

'Did you get his real name?'

She cracked her window open a fraction.

'No, no-names was part of the deal. He said he had this special job for which he wanted a no-questions-asked helicopter and pilot and was prepared to pay for it.

'What story did he give you?'

'Pretty well the one I gave you: that a rich friend was making off with a married woman and needed a fast getaway.'

'And you believed it?'

'Not really because he seemed the sort of horrible little man who couldn't tell the truth if he wanted but, like you, I needed the money.'

'How much?' This wasn't something I needed to know and finding out didn't make me any happier.

'Five thousand; two and a half up front and the rest on completion,' she gave me a sideways glance to check how I was taking this exploitation of my labour, 'but of course, I never got the second half.'

Even so, she'd made a quick thousand over what she'd paid me.

'Not a bad deal, Cress; twenty-five hundred profit for you if everything had worked out.'

She rolled her eyes.

'But it didn't did it? The first I knew that it was all going wrong was when I saw the report of your helicopter blowing up at Cambridge. I felt terrible; those poor policemen.'

'Or poor me, if things had gone to plan. That bomb was set for me to do a Haley's Comet enroute home.'

For just a second her hand touched the back of mine on the gear lever.

'Mike, please believe me when I say I knew nothing of this plan.'

I took my hand away.

'So what did you do about this little disaster you'd created?'

'I didn't know what to do. The papers were full of how the helicopter had been used to pick up Lady Tracam's ransom. I felt like I'd killed her myself.'

'And then Foxy rang you?'

'Yes, that same evening. He told me not to think about going to the police because I was an accessory and would end up in prison myself; said he'd call me the next day about the final payment. He did and you know the rest.'

I nodded.

'Our Foxy friend's a little too ready to settle his accounts explosively. My guess is that it was the reward that decided him to give you the heave-ho. Threats of going to gaol might have kept you from blabbing to the boys in blue but a quarter-million quid almost guaranteed he'd get turned in.'

She shook her head sadly.

'Strangely enough, I didn't even think of it; I was more worried what me going to gaol would do to Robin.'

'Well, I did and I intend to get it.'

'Oh.'

I knew what she was thinking and a few hours ago she would have been dead right but not now.

'Not by handing you in, Cress. I don't think there's much you could tell them anyway. Presumably, you don't know anything else about this Foxy?'

She shook her head.

'Nothing. I had no contact back to him and he insisted you have none back to me...' ,we were in North London now and I was pulling into a cab rank, '...what are you doing?'

'Tying up loose ends.' I went to the first cab and prepaid him to take Sandra's keys and a note telling her where she could pick up the mini plus ten quid to buy some juice. She'd probably feel hurt and betrayed but I'd get her a new one out of the reward. I rejoined Cress in the jeep. 'Right, we're off.'

'Where?'

'How about a wet heath on Hackney marshes?'

Her face was a picture of bewilderment.

'You're joking. What on earth for?'

'You'll see.' I shoved the jeep in first and wheeled away, hoping like hell I would too.

CHAPTER EIGHT

'THIS IS IT?' CRESS sounded dubious and I couldn't blame her.

'This is it.' I tried to sound confident but I was having a mild attack of doubt myself. A soggy North London heath in November was not a place I'd normally bring a girl but this was no normal November, no normal girl and, for this week at least, no normal heath. We sat in the jeep while two hundred yards away, an oasis of coloured lights pulsated to the throb of pipe-organed Strauss.

'A funfair?' Her voice was a mixture of suspicion and bemusement. 'What for? Why?'

I pulled out the piece of scrap *Yellow Pages* with the circled display ad.

'Smallbright's Travelling Funfair; I didn't think this was too significant at first but finally Foxy's personalised number plate gelled and here we are.' I lit yet another cigarette. 'Doesn't look like a bastion of organised crime, does it?'

'Not a bit.' She pulled the anorak on over her blue sweatshirt. 'How did you know they were here anyway?'

'By ringing the number in the ad while you were packing. It turned out to be a booking agency.' Unfortunately, not too many others had followed my example judging by the few cars sharing the temporary carpark. The wind and rain had gone now leaving a clear starlit sky but it was still too bitterly cold to tempt the average punter from his fireside. A pity, because I'd been relying on safety in numbers. 'Might be better if you stayed here, Cress.'

'What, and miss all the fun of the fair.' She released her seatbelt and it flew back on the recoil like a ferret to the warren. 'Come on, you can buy me a hotdog.'

We set off through the archway of coloured lights ahead

of us, the smell of damp heather in seeming contrast to the
roar of generators and the crash of dodgems.

'What are we looking for, exactly?' Cress held the hotdogs
while I dolloped the mustard.

'The Mercedes, Foxy or his mate, perhaps some evidence
that Lady Tracam was actually held here.' I had to raise my
voice above the strains of the *Blue Danube* being pumped out
of the carousel behind us. In faraway Vienna, old Johann was
probably turning in his grave but on Hackney marshes it at
least lent some jollity to the scene.

The same couldn't be said of the funfair staff.

'Heh, Mario, how goes it?' It was a fairground hand and he
was yelling to the carousel's swarthy operator sitting slouched
at his central control. Mario waved back. He wore earings
and his surly features barely concealed the latent savagery I
suspected lay beneath.

'Lovely looking lot, aren't they?'

'Mm, but, just the same, Robin would enjoy all this.' Her
thoughts were obviously far away and that wouldn't do, not
here in the enemy camp.

'Perhaps we'll take him to a proper one someday.' I steered
her away from the carousel with its bucking horses and men-
acing operator, towards the sideshows on the periphery of the
ground. 'Keep your eyes peeled for unfriendly faces.'

'And if we see one?'

'Make sure it doesn't see us and we'll take it from there.'

Just down the line of booths, a signboard outside a small
brightly striped tent caught my attention.

Madam Levoy
Purveyor of Fortunes

Beneath this dubious claim was a big colour photo of
the lady herself looking suitably mystical and incongruously
blonde in her gypsy gear.

'Thinking of having a reading?' Cress was faintly amused.

'No, but I've a feeling I've met Madame Levoy before.'

'Oh, where?'

'I can't remember.' Seeing the seer in the flesh might have jogged the brain cells but it wouldn't be tonight because underneath was a more hastily printed notice:

Madame Levoy regrets no readings until
further notice.

A pity her visions of the future hadn't extended to a date. We wandered on to the next stall.

It was a shooting gallery where a few budding marksmen were trying to impress their girlfriends by knocking down finger targets with airguns; ones with duff sights judging by the dearth of hits. This didn't seem to bother the pimply-faced girl in grimy Stetson doling out pellets and prizes at a ratio of a hundred to one. I called her over.

'Where's Madame Levoy?'

'What, Lena?' the voice was pure Limehouse but certainly friendlier than her colleagues looked, 'she's gone on holiday.'

'How long? She was supposed to give me a reading,' I lied.

She shrugged rounded shoulders.

'Search me; she didn't say.'

'Thanks. Oh, one other thing,' I tried to sound spontaneous, 'does Mr Smallbright still personally run the fair?'

'What, Charlie? Yeh.' These were a lot of questions for one night and suspicion momentarily clouded the pimples. 'Why?'

My turn to shrug.

'Just wondered if it was the same Charlie Smallbright I used to know,' I gave her a fair description of Foxy.

'That's Charlie all right. His caravan's at the other end if you want to see him.' She pointed to the farthest rides but this info wasn't for free. She gave her moneybag a good shake. 'Want to shoot?'

I paid for twelve pellets, found the sighting correction with the first six, knocked down six targets with the second and restored Annie Oakley's smile by waiving the prize.

'So now we have a real name for Foxy.' Cress took my arm as we moved on.

'Sounds like it. Let's have a look at Charlie Smallbright's pad.'

We kept strolling past the assorted stalls and booths and their rough-looking attendants. They were getting meagre pickings tonight and what few punters there were seemed to have gathered round a stage-like booth at the far end. Sheep-like as the rest, we gravitated towards it. Under bright flood-lights in the centre, arms folded over massive bare chest, stood a man. I felt Cress's fingers tighten on my arm.

'Mike!'

'Yeh, I see him.' The fun had just gone out of the fair and for good reason: in the last thirty-six hours the man up there had tried to kill us both. I'd called him the Gorilla but the sign above the booth showed he rejoiced in a grander title.

Mandengo The Invincible

Seeing him now, in the raw, I thought the description was probably pretty accurate. For anyone wanting to test that, a barker beside him was offering fifty pounds reward to anyone staying one round. Much as I liked rewards, I could forego being toe to toe with that hunk of granite.

Not so the lad stepping up onto the stage to the cheer of his mates and Mandengo's sneer. I'd have put more on a brewer's dray winning the National than laddy going ten seconds but it had the rest of the crowd shelling cash for admittance to the ring inside. We wouldn't be joining them and as we cleared the immediate area, Cress gave a visible shudder.

'Ugh, what a horrible man.'

I'd have put it stronger than that but there was one good thing about it.

'At least we know we're in the right place.'

'So why don't we just call the police?'

'With what evidence?' By now we were away from the

main area of the fair amongst the lorries and trailers. I pulled her into the lee of a big multi-wheel transporter. 'By the time we'd convinced the police, any link between here and the kidnapping would be long gone.' I paused to light a cigarette. 'If it's still here at all, I want to get that hard evidence before we go handing ourselves in.'

'....or you go claiming the reward.'

She was right, of course, and I didn't argue but neither did she as I led her off towards the edge of the ground. The residential vans had to be just ahead. From somewhere to our left came the steady rumble of the fair's diesel generators while behind us the strains of Strauss grew ever feinter.

They weren't the only things getting feinter: the bright lighting clusters now sported an opaque misty halo and I realised that clear skies and rapidly cooling heathland were combining to produce that enemy of all pilots: radiation fog. Smallbright's Travelling Funfair was socking in and fast.

I wasn't sure whether this was good or bad for us, but it did add to the atmosphere of latent evil and an awareness that away from the relative safety of the public we had to be infinitely more cautious. Already the thickening night air was beginning to deaden sound but not enough to prevent me hearing approaching footsteps ahead of ours. I stubbed my cigarette, pulled Cress behind a trailer and waited, hardly daring to breathe as they passed.

We needn't have worried; the round-shouldered figure who slouched by was just a youth and a pretty cadaverous sickly-looking specimen at that. Nevertheless, we let him get well clear before breathing again.

'Phew,' Cress ran nervous fingers through her hair, 'this cloak and dagger stuff is wearing me out.'

'Probably just a fairground hand but we'd better keep on the alert from now on.' A few more cautious steps brought us to the last of the transporters and the floodlit misty *laager* of the residential vans.

Most were run-of-the-mill tourers but a couple were big four-wheel, swivel-axle jobs. One in particular stood out; it must have been at least thirty feet long with plenty of decorative art work and chrome. Through the thickening fog, floodlights picked out the gleam of gloss paintwork: lime green, just like the Mercedes parked next to it with the personalised number. I only had time to give Cress a quick glance before I heard the two men approaching.

They came from somewhere on the periphery of the fair, dressed alike in dark green oilskins and woollen hats of the same colour and they knew where they were going too: straight to Charlie Smallbright's flashy van. They looked furtively around to check they were alone and then banged on his door.

From the shadows, we watched as movement appeared behind the curtained windows. Seconds later the door opened to reveal a tall thin figure outlined in the interior light.

Cress squeezed my arm again.

'Foxy.'

'Yeh, alias Charlie Smallbright,' I whispered back, 'owner of this fountain of fun.

Actually there didn't seem to be too much fun in Charlie himself right now. We were thirty yards away and couldn't hear his actual words but it was obvious they were far from welcoming to his unexpected guests. Nevertheless, after a bit of forceful prompting on their part, not to say shoving, he reluctantly allowed them in.

Cress had been peering over my shoulder.

'What's all that about?'

'I don't know but I'd like to find out.' I looked around, frustrated by the glare of the floodlights. 'Too much damn light for me to get close to the window.' In the far background the diesel generator rumbled through the fog. 'I wonder....?'

'Wonder what?'

'You'll see; follow me.'

We headed back towards the main attractions and I noticed there were even fewer punters than when we'd left. Not hard to guess why: everyone was heading homeward before the fog came down with a vengeance. Already, some stalls were shutting up shop. Bad for us both ways: less safety in public numbers and some of the crew would be wandering back to their shells where I wanted to do a bugging job on their boss. I'd have to be quick. I kept us walking towards the source of much of the fair's noise and all of its light.

Not hard to find with the generator roaring out all its fifteen hundred horses into the still night. It was mounted on an open-sided trailer a fair way from the caravans. I didn't blame them; I had to shout in Cress's ear just to make her hear above the din.

'I'm going up for a recce. You stay here and let me know quick if anyone's coming.'

'Do you know what you're doing?' She was cupping her hands to my ear.

'No, but I might when I get up there.' At least I hoped so. No good trying to explain my plan in that racket. I climbed up right next to the roaring beast and did a quick check of its vitals.

On one side was a big red button with STOP printed in large letters above. Obviously the quickest way to get things silenced but also the quickest to restore. I needed something more delayed and permanent. I traced the fuel line from the injectors back to the main tank at the rear. A union nut attached the line to the tank. I tried giving it a turn and found it solid tight.

No tools on the trailer; I felt in my pockets and came out with my apartment keys and a handkerchief. The keys were on a ring fashioned in the shape of a helicopter. I laid the miniature helicopter along the flat of the nut, wrapped and twisted the handkerchief into a tornique around it, took a firm grip and twisted. Nothing. I backed off, flexed my hand to restore circulation and gave it one more try. A deep breath, a renewed grip and then I exhaled and twisted until I thought I'd explode a blood vessel.

Had the union turned or was it just my grip slipping? A second later I felt dampness, smelt fumes and saw diesel fuel, sweet as pure nectar, starting to trickle down the line. I turned the union a few more turns just to make sure it was really free and then backed it up again to finger-tightness.

Cress was still maintaining her lookout but I brought her up and showed her, by sign, the unscrewing of the union. Once again fuel leaked and once again I retightened it. Then I led her down and away from the oppressive heat and noise.

'Cress, I want you to go back there and at exactly 2300 hours....,' we synchronised our watches at 2250, '....I want you to unscrew that union like I just showed you until it's right off the tank and the fuel's running free. Once you've done that, get out and head straight for the jeep. Make sure you don't run into anyone. I'll join you there later. Do you understand?'

She nodded.

'How about you?'

'I'm going to use the next ten minutes to get back to Charlie's. When the engine fails this whole lighting system is going to go quencho quick. That should give me all the darkness and a lot of the diversion I need for a good earwig of what's going on. With a bit of luck the tank will have emptied by the time they suss the trouble so they'll have to refuel too: plenty of time for us to make the getaway.'

'You seem to have it all worked out.' She paused and then gave me a peck on the cheek. 'Be careful.' Then she was gone.

I made it back to Charlie's caravan with minutes to spare but his lights were out already. Either he'd hit the sack or gone out and neither was part of my plan but if he'd gone out it wasn't far because his Merc still stood beside the trailer. Just the same, a new plan was already forming. How about a full nose inside?

This new scheme had to be pretty impromptu because it was now on the stroke of 2300 and any second Cress would be sticking it to the generator. How long would it take to burn the fuel in the line? Not long with the power it kicked out. I checked my watch again: 2302 and all the lights still burning like Blackpool's golden mile.

Another agonising minute ticked its way into eternity

and the diesel kept purring. Horrible doubts were just forming when all eight cylinders died together and with them, every spark of light in the fairground. Good girl, Cress.

Even the carousel must have been electric because the *Blue Danube* flowed slowly to a standstill along with the dodgems. Only the curses of fairground staff and punters broke through a silence that was almost deafening. I wasn't listening. I was already at the back of Charlie's trailer.

I LOOKED FOR AN open window but every one was shut tighter than a bathysphere on pressure test. What now?

In spite of the darkness and confusion already reigning, forcing a window was bound to attract attention and, if Charlie were still inside, stumph my plans completely. Besides, I didn't have any tools. By now, my search had completed a full circle of the van and I stood looking at the most obvious and unlikely possibility of all: the front door. I turned the handle and pulled and, incredibly, the thing opened. I stepped inside and closed it behind me.

For a few seconds I stood immobile, my eyes adjusting to the darkness and wondering why someone so nervous of callers should be so lax on security. I made my cautious way through the van.

Moon and starlight pierced the blinds and curtains and I let their beams guide me through to the far end room. Through the open door I glimpsed an empty double bed but no Charlie Smallbright. I retraced my way through the van to the room at the other end which I hoped was his office. I knew I had to be quick: if he'd left the trailer unlocked, then his absense would only be short. It was probably only the power failure that had stopped him returning already. When that was restored I'd have light, Charlie, his gang and big trouble in that order. The door to the office was wide open and in the moonlight I saw the safe.

It was hard up against the far wall, its door ajar. I knelt in front, pulled it wide and looked. No papers, no money and no evidence of the kidnapping; just some powder, two plastic kilo bags of the stuff, and on the shelf above, some small sachets of the same. I thought of the wasted-looking youth that we'd seen slouching away a half-hour earlier; Smallbright's Travelling Funfair was obviously dispensing more than fun and frolic as it toured the country.

Kidnapping, drug dealing, murder; these were evil men and here, in the centre of their camp I felt a little weasel of unease making his icy-footed way up my backbone. I knew why: I'd been stupid enough to head straight for that open safe without so much as a glance at the rest of that darkened room. Now something told me I'd regret it.

Slowly, I turned round until my eyes fell on the desk partly hidden on entry by the open door. The desk faced me. More disconcerting still, so did the man sitting behind it.

CHAPTER NINE

HE SAT STILL AND silent with his head seemingly made of glass. It was only a fleeting impression because already I was diving for the floor and rolling twice to avoid the hot lead I was sure would be imminently flying. In the silent darkness, the sound was like a thunderclap.

Not the crack of a pistol but the roar of the generator re-starting down-site. With it came the fairground lights, filling the van with a multi-coloured glow as the diesel settled into a steady rumble. It was more than could be said for my heart. A quick deep breath and then I shakily brought my line of sight back above the rim of the desk.

I'd been worrying about two things returning: the light and Charlie Smallbright. Now the one cancelled the other because in the eerie rainbow glow I could see that Charlie would never be a worry again.

He sat in his desk chair, wrists tied to the arms like a can-didate for the big fry at Sing-Sing. That would have been an easier route to go than the one they'd given him. Having your head stuffed into a polythene bag and slowly suffocating can't be the best way to pop your clogs; not if Charlie's protruding tongue and organ-stopped eyes were anything to go by.

I didn't waste time trying to figure out why and even less on sympathy. If my position had been dodgy before it was downright precarious now. Three minutes was all I now gave myself to find something useful and get out.

I started working my way through his desk drawers with those protruding vacuum-packed eyes watching my every move. The lower drawers were locked but a bit of revolting fishing through the dead man's pockets produced the keys. Charlie should have left those drawers unlocked: the forty-five automatic I found in the lower right might have saved

him that last view of his assailants through single-ply neo-
prene. I left it where I found it; I'd enough problems without
being caught in possession of a murdered man's shooter. Beneath the gun was a blue soft-covered book.

TIDE TABLES - LANGSDEN PRIORY STAITHE

Their reason was explained by a small framed photo atop
the desk: an old sailing boat, a sea-going job by the look of it
in which Charlie had doubtless mixed a little business with
pleasure. I took the back off the frame, put the photo between
the pages of the tide-tables and stuffed them into my jacket
pocket. Something to go on; time to go.

I quickly wiped everywhere I'd managed to put my sticky
prints, cracked the front door open a half inch and peeked
outside. If there were people about, I couldn't see them because in the few minutes I'd been ageing ten years inside, the
fog had thickened to pea soup. Wrapped in its obscuring blanket, I left the van and made my cautious way through the fair
towards the carpark and Cress. Not as fast as I would have
liked because I kept having to stop and check my bearings.

No sound to guide me now either; the combination of
fog and blackout had expedited the few remaining punters
on their homeward way leaving the fair still and silent. Using
my sense of direction, I crept onward and shortly the ghostly
forms of white horses and red-striped poles told me I'd found
the Carousel. I quickened my step; apart from a few muffled
voices through the clag, so far I hadn't met a soul.

With so little way to go I could have afforded to be extra
cautious, quietened my own footsteps and listened for others. Instead I hurried on and half-way round the Carousel ran
headlong into a man.

It would have been a nerve-jolter at the best of times but
these weren't the best of times and this wasn't the best of men
either. It was my old friend, the Gorilla.

• • •

I DIDN'T KNOW WHICH of us was the more shocked but the sickly smile of recognition that spread across his ugly potato face told me who was the more pleased. I could guess what was going through what passed for his brain: this time two hundred pounds of granite muscle would succeed where a pound of Semtex had failed.

Not if I could help it. With only speed and manoeuvrability on my side, I went to outflank him.

The Gorilla's massive bulk was deceptive; years in the ring had made him no slouch and with dismaying ease he blocked my way with a smile that in an instant turned from sinister to downright sadistic. I knew why when those leg-sized arms locked round my torso.

The pressure was akin to being crushed by an Anaconda. I tried a few feeble punches to his face but I might as well have been splashing water for all the effect they had. The life-deadening pressure built from plain agonising to hyper-excruciating while his smile never slipped a millimetre. My vision was reddening, there was ringing in my ears; I had to do something quick or the next sound would be the snap of my own spine. I summoned the last dregs of remaining strength and brought my knee up right between his rock-hard thighs.

He didn't let go but it took the smile off his face, a little pressure from his arms and a globule of oxygen back into my starved lungs. It was enough to give me a boost of resolution. I crossed my thumbs under his nose, forced back his bullet head and gave another upward jab of the knee that should have rung the changes on his tonsils.

I didn't hear them but only because, as his massive arms fell away completely, he gave a bellow that would have stampeded a herd of elephants. I'd have run too if I could but after that gargantuan gut-bust, the most I could manage was a pathetic drunken stagger.

It wasn't enough. He came after me at a pace unbelievable for his titanic bulk, let alone my efforts to lift his voice six octaves. I'd hurt him because his face still had a look of tight-lipped agony but that only made the prospect of him getting those metal-benders on me again something to definitely avoid. I sheered off the only way open: direct across the Carousel.

It was a tactical as well as desperate move. He must have been twice my size and I'd hoped manoeuvring between the red-saddled horses would slow him down. Also, in the central control booth, there might be something, anything, that I could use as a weapon. I plunged into the booth with its silent control desk and found the something was nothing and Gorilla right behind me. By the time I'd wasted seconds on a fruitless search he was blocking the doorway with a sickly smile that gave some indication of the vengeance now to come.

There was no escape this time and almost casually, he gave me a one-handed push backwards into the booth. It must be how he'd bounced many a victim off the ringropes except I didn't bounce, I went dead-backed into the operating console with a force that rattled my kidneys on just about every button, knob and lever on the panel. Lights came on, there was a whirring somewhere below and instantly the whole contraption started working and turning. Inside the booth, I was about ready to be torn limb from limb but out there coloured lights flashed, wooden horses pranced and the speakers boomed out Straus's *Radetzky-Marsch*. The Gorilla smiled again, picked me up by my jacket lapels and lifted me bodily outside.

I tried another upward kick but he wasn't going to be caught a third time; before my flailing legs came within a gasp of his midships he'd swung me up and downwards in a spine-busting back-slam straight onto the unyielding boards of the ride. Through a haze of semi-consciousness I saw only the vast bulk of his two hundred and fifty plus pounds coming down in a kneedrop right onto my chest. It was a pile-driving force that just about blew my guts through the top of my head but what little resistance did remain, he now proceeded to wring out with his hands round my throat.

I kicked my legs and flailed my fists into his face but he

was oblivious. I was like a moth pinned to the collector's board, spread-eagled on the centre island with my head actually bouncing on the rotating turntable of the ride. Above, the coloured lights spun ever faster while the thump of the organ competed with a steam-like roar in my ears. I was going quickly and I knew it.

CHAPTER TEN

GORILLA KNEW IT TOO and he was going to make the most of it before my thumping heart kicked its last. The smile widened to a grin and I noticed for the first time that he had rotten teeth and bad breath. On the smooth deck of the ride, I groped blindly, searching for anything I could use to knock those black stumpy teeth down his halitosis-breathing throat. As I twisted and turned I felt a sharp pain in my left thigh: my apartment keys stabbing through the pocket.

I groped feverishly with my left hand, using those last desperate seconds to drag them out and take as firm a grip of the helicopter fob as my dwindling strength allowed. It was now or never and never would last an eternity. I jabbed the small helicopter right into his vile puffy face.

All the despair of a doomed man went into that lunge and if he'd kept his head still I'd have put a gash down his cheek six inches long. Instead he saw it coming, instinctively ducked and put the miniature rotor straight into his eye.

For the second time that night I felt his deadly grip loosen but there was no bellow of pain this time, just a scream of excruciating agony and I could see why: the rotor was jammed right into the socket. He grabbed it mindlessly and pulled and out it came together with a good portion of eyeball and a spurt of aqueous fluid.

Pretty catastrophic for him but bliss to my throat and lungs. He was kneeling beside me now, blubbering away with his hands over a rapidly spreading sheet of crimson but even a hulk like Gorilla can only take so much agony. Like a poleaxed bull, he slowly but surely toppled sideways right onto the ride.

With wooden horses prancing above him, he went curving away while I dragged some heathland air down my abused windpipe. By the time he came round on his first circuit I'd got to my knees, still gasping tortured breaths but at least breathing.

That was more than Gorilla would ever do again. When he'd rolled onto the ride his big head must have gone under one of the plunging wooden hooves and that's where it was now, being pummelled to ever bloodier pulp with each beat of the *Radetzky*. This was one Humpty who'd never be put together again.

Time to go. I looked out into the enveloping fog and saw the ghostly figures of other funfair staff begin to materialise. Perhaps they'd already found Smallbright. Even if they hadn't, by the time they saw the bloody splodge that had been Gorilla's head their feelings for me would be a long hike from benevolent. Fighting off waves of nausea, I pulled myself to my feet and just as quickly realised I was going nowhere. I was still only half-mobile from my bashing and already the first of the staff had reached the ride. Amongst them was Mario, the evil-looking thug who ran the thing and as he climbed aboard something flashed in his hand. A knife. Once again I backed away onto the turning ride.

He came stalking after me amongst the bucking nags and the distance between us narrowed by the second. He'd spent his working life on this thing and was in his element whereas my life seemed destined to end on it. Above the thudding beat of the *Radetzky* I never even heard her coming.

The first I saw were twin orb-like eyes piercing their smoky way through the fog. Then they materialised into Cress's stocky little buggy with its top down and her at the wheel. I wasn't sure which looked the more beautiful as they came bouncing through the ground, straight towards the Carousel.

I didn't care either because Mario was now just two horses away and all set for a bit of live dissection while more of the swarthy clan came anti-clockwise to cut off my retreat. That might not be all they'd cut off unless.....

I'd had some good wingmen in the past but none to compare with Cress Dysart that night as she brought her little

blue bomber formating right alongside while I tried desperately to keep an arm's length between me and knife-toting
Mario. She was half-standing in her seat now, not slackening
a knot, gunning round with the ride and scattering miscellaneous fairground hands in the process. Above the racket of
the organ she yelled two words.

'Mike....jump!'

I didn't need a second telling; as Mario's blade scythed
downwards I took a flying leap, landed with one leg inside
the jeep and the rest of my battered hulk outboard, clinging
to the roll-bar while Cress hit the gas and saved herself some
tyre wear by making the last half-circuit on two wheels. She
straightened between two booths and then we were headed for
the gate, a blind swerving run between misty images emerging
from the ten-metre visibility with me all the time trying to
swing myself onboard like some demented Cossack.

I'd just about made it when we went zinging under the
arched gateway and bouncing down the rough track towards
the main road. Far astern, Smallbright's Travelling Funfair
vaporised into the fog and was gone. By the time we reached
the main road I'd made the front seat beside her. She turned
briefly.

'Which way?'

'Left....north-east....pick up the M.11.' She gave me a
questioning look but complied just the same.

A good job she did. We'd just turned when a wailing siren
pierced the fog followed, seconds later, by a blue flasher casting eerie reflections through the vapour as a police car came
speeding from the south to swing purposely into the fairground
track. Hard to believe anyone there had called the law but
someone had and the boys in blue were going to find plenty
to make their trip worthwhile: a couple of still-warm corpses
with a safeful of hot dope thrown in for good measure.

They'd find something else too: a bloodied keyring with a
helicopter fob and I doubted it would take them long to work
out whose locks those keys fitted.

If I'd been a suspect before, I'd be Public Enemy Number One before this long night was through.

'GOOD GRIEF, TEMPEST, NEVER get into politics. You'd have us in World War Three before your maiden speech.'

Away from the London basin the fog had disappeared, the motorway at this hour, almost deserted. We were gobbling the northbound miles at a fair rate and I'd just finished giving Cress the complete rundown on my fun-filled hour at Smallbright's. Her reaction was pretty rich, considering she'd got me into this miasma in the first place but I didn't remind her. Not yet anyway, I was still too grateful.

'Thanks for the rescue, Cress.'

She turned and smiled.

'That's okay. You seemed to be taking an awfully long time and I guessed you'd be hot-footing it when you did so I occupied myself taking the hood off. It makes things a lot quicker.' She glanced up at the canvas top now back in place. Fresh air was all very well but in controllable quantities and we'd stopped and rerigged the thing just before hitting the M.11, 'When I heard the Carousel start up again I guessed something was wrong, eased down to the entrance for a look and saw you about to be perforated by that horrible Mario.' Her smile had a hint of mischief. 'It seemed a good time to repay what I owed you.'

'Amen to that.' Bracing feet and shoulders, I rolled my old bone-bag into another position. I was trying to be fair and give equal exposure but inevitably some of the bruises screamed discrimination. 'Do you want me to drive?'

'No, I'm okay and you need a rest.' She drove silently for another mile but when she spoke again there was almost despair in her voice. 'Mike, what are we getting into here? We went to that crazy fair tonight to find the man who murdered Lady Tracam and found him murdered instead. We wanted some questions answered and instead, raised even more. We wanted to clear your name and now you're more on the run than ever. What's this all about?'

'Drugs, by the look of it.' I lit another cigarette, thankful that at least my lungs were up to a bit more abuse. 'I'm sure Smallbright has been smuggling the stuff in that boat of his and using the fair as a front for distribution around the country.'

'So why kidnap Lady Tracam?'

'Probably a simple case of evil breeding evil. That's a pretty murderous crew back there and I wouldn't put anything past them.'

'Who murdered Smallbright then?' She cranked her window a half inch and vented some of my blue heaven over the Essex landscape.

I shrugged.

'Who knows; perhaps a rival gang whose territory he was muscling in on. He seemed to know those two woolly-hat types who snuffed him.'

'Nothing to do with the kidnapping?'

'I can't see how unless the underworld felt he'd over-extended himself and brought too much agro down on everyone.' I did another painful reallocation of bruises on the unyielding seat.' Those two hatchet men looked a bit nautical to me. Perhaps they're connected with the Norfolk end. I'm sure the kidnapping was somehow. Remember my first pickup was up on the North Norfolk coast.'

'Which is why we're heading up there now.' The gap in the window was blowing her hair. It was two a.m. but her concentration was intact, driving steady, questions incisive. 'To find what?'

'The boat. A connection. The truth.' We were pulling off the motorway now to pick up the A.11. 'The truth is all I've got going for me now, Cress, but after tonight I've a feeling the law will regard it as ever less relevant.'

'Unless we can prove otherwise first,' she swung off the

roundabout and picked up the A road for the coast, 'but don't forget we're dealing with a killer.'

Killer. To her it was an adjective but to me, a repellent noun that dragged my mind back seventeen hours to Battersea and decades to an even blacker past. We drove on in silence, my thoughts a tumbling maelstrom. I hadn't wanted reminding of O-Kane but at least it had clicked in my sub-conscious recall: I remembered now where before I'd seen Madam Le-Voy, the blonde seer of Hackney Marshes.

Our old friend, the fog, returned as we neared the coastal belt of North Norfolk and it was six a.m. when we finally checked into a motel on the outskirts of the village of Langsden Priory.

THERE ARE FEW PROBLEMS in this world that can't at least be eased by a few gallons of steaming atomised water sluicing over your torso. I'd got a lot of problems and it took a lot of water but in the end I emerged from the shower with brain soothed and bruises bright. I pulled on my jeans and joined Cress, towelling as I went.

'Hmm, you look almost human.' She was lying on the double bed wrapped in a huge bath towel. In a fit of gallantry I'd given her first shot at the shower, 'How are the aches and pains?'

'Being endured with heroic fortitude in trying circumstances.'

In fact the only thing trying about my present circumstances was staying out of that bed. The motel owner hadn't asked why two grotty jeep-freaks should be pleading for a room at daybreak but if he'd had suspicions, they were groundless. In our shattered state, we'd simply crashed onto the bed fully dressed and slept the sleep of the just until late morning. Now, refreshed and revived, I think we both sensed the latent sexuality of our situation but I confined my move to the bed to sitting on its edge.

'How about you?'

'All the better for this coffee; here's yours?' She passed over a steaming mug and rolled over onto one arm facing me. 'Okay, Skipper; what's the plan?'

The towel was doing a lousy job of covering her lean calves but I resisted the temptation for innuendo and took a swig of instant instead.

'The plan is for me to take your jeep, drive into Langsden Priory and find Smallbright's yacht.'

'I'll come with you.'

I shook my head.

'No, Cress, I want you to stay here and try and contact Sir John Tracam. Give him a run-down on what's happened and say we're just tying up loose ends but that we need his legal help with the law before we come into the open.'

'What about you; don't you need more sleep?'

That bed was calling like a *siren* and not just for sleep.

'No, it's late as it is. I'll get going and sort this thing out once and for all.' I got up wincing, half with the pain of sudden movement, half at the boredom of my resolution. At the same time I saw myself in the mirror and the only consolation it gave was that no-one was going to recognise me from the police description in the papers. The marks around my neck looked like the collar of some satanic cleric.

'At least let me get something to rub into those bruises.'

'Later.' I pulled on the rest of my days-stale wardrobe, grabbed jeep and motel keys off the bedside table, went to leave, thought twice, came back and gave her a kiss. 'Thanks anyway.'

A soft hand stroked the side of my face.

'Be careful.'

'I'll try.'

On past performance, not a promise to hang on but as much as I could manage as I forced myself out into that cold Norfolk air.

I should have told her to be careful too. I really should.

CHAPTER ELEVEN

THE RUN FROM THE motel was short on distance and long on time. High pressure was still lingering over the south of England and the fog with it. Here in the low marshy coastal stretches visibility was down to a few hundred metres. I drove slowly, signpost-hopping down the narrow lanes to Langsden Priory.

It was gone midday when I finally came cruising into the village, only to find that Langsden Priory Staithe was a separate hamlet a quarter mile further on. Much smaller than its parent, it consisted of just a few flint cottages scattered around a small quay; quite pretty if you were in the mood. I wasn't.

I drove onto the quay and parked outside the chandlers. Out in the creek, fast drying on the ebb tide, were remnants of the summer fleet: the odd sailing and power cruiser, one modern fishing boat and a couple of traditional Cromer crabbers. Nothing resembling the photo in my pocket but that didn't mean Charlie's old lugger wasn't there; fog hid the outer reaches of the creek and the sea itself, unseen beyond the desolate salt marshes. A bell clanged as I opened the chandler's door.

Inside was the usual Aladdin's Cave of ropes, flags, brass fittings and nautical clothing but no customers. The man I took to be the proprietor glanced up from amending some charts and took off his specs.

'Can I help you?'

The Norfolk accent was friendly enough. I showed him the photo. He re-popped his specs and studied it closely, nodding.

'That's the old *JUSTAFINA*, ex-beach yawl decked over. Her owner's a bit of a rough diamond... also bought the old beach company sheds and that's where she's moored.'

'Beach Company? What's that?'

The chandler gave a knowing laugh.

'Old history. The beach companies were the boys who did most of the salvage work on this coast round the turn of the century. The beginnings of the lifeboat service in a way though some says them big yawls was more intent on cargoes than saving life.' He shook himself out of the romantic past and back to the mundane present. 'Anyway, the Langsden Priory company's old sheds and lookout are out on the point.' He took off his specs again. 'Quite a way from here; are you driving or walking?'

'Walking.'

At the door he pointed to a pathway running in front of the few cottages looking out over the creek.

'Follow that for about a half mile and it'll bring you to an unmade track running down to the sheds. A good four miles all told.'

I left the jeep on the quay and got striding; a brisk walk would loosen my aching joints and get me a lot closer to the sheds unseen than blasting multi-horsepower up to the front door. If I did meet trouble I had the fog still curling off the salt marshes to give me cover.

It was a pleasant walk at first with the path well-maintained and even boarded in places where the ground was soft. There were few houses and apart from the wraithlike shape of the odd horse wandering out of the murk, I was alone with my thoughts.

There were plenty of those: trying to give some order to the crazy kaleidoscope of the last few days and my changing feelings for Crestovana Dysart. Enemy to ally or was it me changing sides as I S-turned along the line of legality. As yet, I hadn't told her about Killer O-Kane, his past, my place in it or how he'd flown Lena LeVoy out of Battersea. There were a lot of odd-shaped pieces to this jigsaw. I was still struggling to see the big picture when I hit the track.

It was shingle and pretty noisy underfoot so I kept to the muddy edge and accepted gunged trainers in exchange for silence, a good move as it turned out because the thickening fog so hid the sheds that I near enough walked right into them.

They were the ramshackle collection of buildings I'd more or less been expecting: a low-roofed, black-tarred main shed surrounded by outbuildings and the usual nautical miscellany of discarded crab pots, floats, chains and barnacle encrusted anchors. The lookout tower stood at one end, a reminder of salvage days and the shades of those who'd once manned it. That it was manned again was evidenced by an old van parked between the sheds and a coil of black coal-smoke climbing from the main building's battered stovepipe.

I hadn't expected habitation and instinctively I edged away from the sheds towards the creek. Warped to the banks was an old sailing boat, her stocky clinkered hull lying well over on the fast-drying mud. She had two masts, a flaking white paint job and on her bows a name: *JUSTAFINA*.

What now? I needed to get inside that shed but it was the same dilemma as the fairground with no generator to conveniently scupper this time. I decided to at least try for a look through the windows. Injun-like, I crept around the shed's black weathered walls, my every step crunching horribly on the pebbles and my heart thumping even louder.

It was hardly worth it; bars and furniture blocked every window. I paused and took in the desolate setting; it wasn't difficult to see the attraction of this bleak outpost to evil industry. Drugs could be smuggled ashore here and stored for short periods with little fear of discovery. Humans too; I was sure this was where Lady Tracam had spent her last terrible days. I moved on to the seaward end of the shed where big double doors led down a natural shingle slipway to low water. I'd taken two steps to pass the doors when they started to open. The only available cover were some fish boxes piled waist high against the front corner. I dived behind them.

A half-second later the men came out, two of them, rough looking thugs from the same mould as the fairground. One was talking into a handheld radio. I caught the words "All clear here." and then they stopped at the top of the shingle slip looking seaward and listening. I listened too and heard the distant purr of high-revving engines.

They came out of the fog like longships from a lost world: two semi-rigid inflatables with two crew each and outboards on their transoms that could have kicked them up to forty knots but idling now for low speed and low noise. Fifty yards out, they cut them completely and ghosted onto the slip with the covert expertise of trained commandos. The crews jumped out and pulled the boats higher up the slip.

If these were drug smugglers, they were in a class of their own. They were dressed alike in short deck boots, dark green oilskins and wool hats. I'd seen that rig before and knew they were experts at more than boat handling. They moved now as a well-trained team with athletic co-ordination and barely a word of command. Under the oilskins, I imagined their physiques as fine tuned as their engines. There was some muttered conversation that I couldn't catch but I did the accent.

It was the unmistakable lilting burr of the Irish.

BY COMPARISON, THE TWO thugs slouching down the slipway to meet them seemed like rejects from Hell's Angel. There was a short and patently insincere exchange of greetings; the boat crews were in a hurry and there was work to be done.

In each boat were long wooden boxes and these were now carried up the slip and into the shed, effortlessly on the shoulders of the commandos and awkwardly shared between the stumbling, cursing thugs.

What was in them? Drugs? Too big for that and with those accents I was pretty sure I knew anyway. Confirmation came quicker than I thought when, halfway up the slip, the thugs dropped their second box, shattering one of its sides and spilling the contents onto the shingle.

Weapons, half a dozen Kalashnikov AK47 automatic rifles, lay gleaming in the filtered sunlight while the two thugs stared dumbly and the lead commando channelled a mountain of fury into one unfeigned word.

'Fool!'

'Don't worry, Mick,' the thug was trying to keep things casual, 'we can stick'm in one of these boxes here.' He came over and grabbed hold of the fishbox behind which I crouched.

'Leave it, you idiot,' the leader's command was sharp and music to my frozen ears, 'I don't want them stinking of rotten fish.' He nodded towards the scattered Kalashnikovs. 'Just get them inside before you do any more damage.'

The thug let go the box with little goodwill on his part but buckets on mine. The loose weapons and remaining boxes were soon in the shed and the boat's crews ready to leave but the lead thug had a question.

'When do we get our money?'

The senior commando paused as he slipped his boat.

'Tonight. Our officer will be here to meet the final load and pay you then.'

'He'd better.'

Perhaps it had been the civility in the commando's tone or the fact that he was in a hurry and leaving that had made the thug chance his luck at bolshiness. Whichever, it was a mistake. The senior commando resecured his RIB and came back to the thug who instinctively took one pace backward. I could understand why because the commando towered over him and his words carried all the hardness of one who can back up every threat he makes.

'Little man, you really aren't in good enough shape to talk like that.' Like a headmaster admonishing a boy, he gave the thug a head-jerking slap across the face, turned on his heel, and jumped back aboard the RIB. He was about to shove off when some little Irish demon made him pause and ask, 'Where's your boss then? I thought he was to be here.'

The thug rubbed his face, kicking some pebbles and keeping his eyes down.

'Couldn't make it; somethin' came up.'

Too true it had and they both knew why.

'Ah, too bad.' There was more than a hint of mockery in the commando's voice and thrown salute. 'till high water then.'

The RIBs drifted out into the stream, started engines and were gone, soon lost in the freezing but fast-thinning fog.

Time for me to be gone too before it thinned anymore and I got caught on the track with no cover. With the two thugs back inside and the big doors closed behind them, I started retracing my steps around the shed. At its inland corner I was about to make my break for the track when the small door on that end opened.

I ducked back around the side as the lead thug came out. He was still rubbing a rather red side to his face and holding a mobile phone to the ear on the other, talking little but nodding a lot. I couldn't hear the words but it was obvious he was getting orders. After pocketing the mobile, he yelled for his cohort locked the shed and soon both were driving away in the old van down the fast-clearing track. I watched them disappear, thankful it wasn't a minute later and free now to recce the place more fully.

I went over to the lookout tower. It was open but containing nothing more than discarded boat gear, a couple of drums of marine diesel, a tapped drum of engine-oil and a box of cotton waste. Back at the shed, I made a circuit trying doors only to confirm every one was locked. Some heavy work at one of the windows might have got me inside but I'd seen and heard enough to know what was going on and breaking and entering would only warn them off. Handing this little set-up over to the authorities should establish my own innocence and, with connection to the Tracam kidnapping, get me the reward from Sir John. With nothing more to be gained, I headed for the track and jog-trotted down the shingle.

It was late-afternoon now with the shadows of evening closing as fast as the fog was clearing. The chief gun-runner had said they'd be back at high water. Low water had been noon so they'd be sliding those RIBs back down the creek about six. That would be the time to grab them, their "officer" and the pickup group.

That left only hours to convince the police and get things

organised. That probably wouldn't be enough. After the events of Wednesday and last night I had the feeling that the boys-in-blue would be more inclined to arrest first and listen afterwards and by then it would be too late anyway. All my hope lay in Cress having contacted Sir John Tracam. If I could talk to him as soon as I got back to the motel, his influence could still get the ball rolling in time. I sped my trot to a run and pressed on.

There was always the chance of the thugs returning so it was a relief to reach the end of the track. I paused just long enough to get my breath back and a bearing from the main road for vehicular access. Then I set off again along the path, running as fast as forty a day would allow and dropping back to a fast walk only when the first buildings of Langsden Priory Staithe hove into view.

By the time I reached the jeep, dusk had turned to darkness with a slight breeze signalling an end to the anti-cyclone and more wind and rain to come. I fired up the jeep and a cigarette together and headed back motelwards. Driving along those undulating unlit lanes, I passed only one set of lights but I did find myself enjoying a little glow inside that I hadn't known for a long time. It could have been satisfaction at good results from the day's recce but in truth I knew it was the thought of Cress waiting there for me, perhaps even worrying about me. Could I be.....?

I turned into the motel carpark to find a good sprinkling of cars; probably evening diners at the restaurant. If all went well, we'd go there ourselves for a celebration later. I let myself into our unit, surprised that the lights were off.

'Good evening, Tempest.' The voice was rough, hard and cold as an iceberg. Not a voice I recognised but I did the figure now materialising in the feint light from the carpark. He was a long way from his Carousel but Mario had ensured this renewal of our previous brief acquaintance would avoid the need for close contact. Once again metal glinted in his hand but this time it was the late-Charlie's significantly deadlier

Colt forty-five automatic. With a design going back almost a century, the forty-five certainly isn't the ultimate in modern small-arms weaponry but that was little consolation to me with its thirty-nine ounces of blued metal aimed straight at my chest.

CHAPTER TWELVE

'CLOSE THE DOOR BEHIND you and move very slowly.'

I did as ordered while a second dark figure came from behind. There was no sign of Cress and I didn't ask, hoping she was out and safe. A forlorn hope. Mario smiled.

'Just in case you're thinking of doing something stupid, Tempest, we have the girl.'

He didn't have to say anymore; there was a hardness in his eyes that only confirmed my original impression that this was a man who would kill without hesitation. Instead, I asked a question.

'How did you find us?'

Mario tapped the side of his nose.

'Not for you to know, Tempest, but let's just agree you're not as clever as you thought.' He leaned forward until the forty-five was inches from my guts. 'You're going to pay for what you did to Charlie-boy and Mandengo.'

It wasn't the time to point out that only one of those was mine. Instead I nodded towards the sounds of music and laughter coming from the restaurant.

'Bit public isn't it?'

'Not here, Tempest,' the grin returned, 'we're going to take a little ride to somewhere nice and secluded.'

'The same place you held and killed Lady Tracam?'

Mario's eyes told me what his voice didn't.

'Never you mind. Just concentrate on walking out of here nice and quiet to that buggy of yours and drive away like a Zombie at a funeral. Any tricks and it's the girl who'll pay for it.'

The music and laughter from within the restaurant were in sombre contrast to the cold blackness of the carpark. No-one saw us leave, Mario beside me jamming a little forty-five-

calibre encouragement into my ribs and the other following
in a car behind. I glanced into the mirror, recognised it as the
late-Charlie's lime-green Mercedes and cursed myself for a
blind fool not spotting it when I arrived. Mario was wrong on
another point: I didn't think I was clever at all and even less
so now I'd led a special girl back into the enemy's clutches.

ONCE AGAIN, I FOLLOWED the meandering way to Langsden Priory, trying hard to stay cool and remember the run of the road
ahead. I had the germ of an idea but it would take a straight
stretch of road, some downward incline and a lot of luck.

I glanced again in the mirror; the Mercedes was about
two car lengths behind. To steady my nerves, I pondered on
what had happened and realised that call to the thugs at the
point had been from Mario ordering them to the motel to
pick up Cress. It was their van I must have passed in the darkness. She'd been that close. I put aside self-recrimination and
concentrated again on the road ahead; we were climbing a
shallow hill now, the last before the village.

We breasted the hill, my hand down by the gears and the
long straight run down to Langsden Priory stretching ahead.
I squeezed in more power and down we accelerated with the
speedo climbing swiftly to seventy and the lights of the following Mercedes dropping momentarily astern.

'Ease off,' Mario's order carried a sneer as the forty-five
jammed harder into my ribs, 'you'll never outrun him.'

I knew that but in seconds I'd be outrunning the hill. I
slid my hand from the gear lever to the socket of his seatbelt.
I'd remembered how fierce was the harness recoil but was it
that way every time? Now was the time to find out. I hit the
release button and the belt flew out like an arrow from the
bow. I caught only a glimpse of Mario's startled look as the
latch flew past his face but in that micro-second of distraction
I hit the brakes hard, the wheels locked and that little bug
screeched to a halt with all the deceleration of a carrier jet
taking the wire.

Not everything stopped: without a seatbelt, the man next

to me kept on going, through the windshield, off the bonnet and down the road ahead, a flailing tumbling bundle of bloodied villainy. Alongside, there was more screeching as the Mercedes went skidding into the far ditch, to stop twenty yards on, heeled thirty degrees to starboard with the offside door jammed in the hedgerow. I could see the driver already scrambling up the front passenger seat.

That took time though and time was something he couldn't afford because while he was still clambering I was already out and retrieving Mario's forty-five. I pulled open the Mercedes' door, smiled briefly and put one quick round straight into the driver's skull. He went back down behind the wheel, very heavily, very still and very dead.

I went back to the jeep, used the weapon to smash out the bloodied remains of the windshield, lit a quick cigarette and drove off. Mario's still form lay just ahead. There was a double bump as the wheels went over him. Ten minutes later they were spitting shingle as I forged seaward up the boatshed track. On either side the salt marshes gleamed black and sinister in the spasmodic moonlight.

I STOPPED TWO HUNDRED yards short of the sheds, safetied the forty-five, jammed it into my jacket pocket and jog-trotted the last stretch hoping the rising wind would blanket the crunch underfoot.

The dark sheds looked ghostlike in the scudding moonlight. I crept into their shadows, wondering if a lookout at the track entrance had put the hands on alert. No reception committee so, presumably, no lookout. After the action back down the road my blood was up enough to go bang on the front door and blast whoever answered it but I was sure Cress was inside and I shied away from turning the place into Dodge City.

The alternative was to get them out; not easy with the temperature turning rapidly arctic and them in the snugness of the shed with oil lamps burning and the stove feeding the fug. The coal stove; I looked up at the blackened chimney belching smoke into the night and headed for the lookout tower. Inside, I rummaged through the box of cotton waste until I found some uncut sheets and old towels. I pulled them out and some of the rags, soaked the latter in engine oil from the tapped drum and went back to the shed.

The roof was pretty low anyway and a waterbut at one corner gave me the needed step. I threw the linen up onto the felt and quickly followed, the creaks and groans lost in the rising wind that was rattling everything that was loose anyway. I sat astride the peak alongside the belching stack.

To help it belch a little more I dropped the oil-soaked rags down the pipe. Black smoke billowed upwards but not for long as I jammed in the sheets and towels. Soon there was not so much as a puff outside.

Results were quick and predictable. I was still easing down the roof when the door below flew open and out came the leading thug, spitting smoke and invective in equal measure. Like a fighter pilot of old, height gave me the initiative; I launched myself off the roof onto his back and he went down gasping with me on top

He didn't gasp for long; the blue-metalled muzzle of the forty-five on the side of his head took care of that. I jumped back to my feet and flattened against the door frame ready for his mate. He soon followed, one hand holding a cloth to his face and the other a belted Smith and Wesson thirty-eight special. My own piece in his beer gut showed that was the best place to leave it.

'Hands behind your head.' He complied while I pulled his weapon and nodded towards the door. 'Inside.'

It was like hell's kitchen. They'd thrown a bucket of water over the stove and oily smoke and steam filled the room. As it vented outside I saw a half-eaten meal on a rough table, the piled boxes of weaponry unloaded that morning and, sitting on them with her hands tied behind, a girl: Cress, white-faced, coughing smoke and fumes but still alive.

'Are you okay?' A stupid question as I half-kneeled behind her, untying the cords, my eyes and the forty-five never leaving the second-thug's guts.

'Yes, I think so.' It was a lie though because, as she massaged painful blood back into her hands, I noticed one of those big blue eyes was now ringed in black.

'Who did that?'

She nodded towards second-thug whose twitching face showed he was already regretting it. He'd made a lot of mistakes tonight but on this he was correct: he'd regret it all right. I stuck the forty-five into my back pocket, grabbed him by his grotty sweatshirt and slammed a fist straight into one of his eyes. As he sank groaning I butted his head into one of the weapons boxes for good measure. He didn't groan anymore.

Cress shook her head.

'You didn't have to do that, Mike.'

'Yes I did.' I fished out the jeep keys and tossed them across to her. 'It's two hundred yards back down the track. Double down there, bring it back and pick me up. You'll find the other beauty lying outside; if he's moving give another swipe with this.' She looked at the Smith and Wesson like I'd just fished it from the sewers but took it just the same and went on her way.

I used the time to have a quick scout around the shed, looking for any evidence of Lady Tracam and finding nothing. It didn't matter; what did was alerting the law to tonight's second drop. The jeep crunched to halt outside. I ran out and jumped in beside Cress.

'Okay, let's head for the nearest phonebox.'

She didn't move but gave me a strange sort of pleading look from the corner of her eyes.

'Come on, Cress; what's the matter?'

'Mike!' She turned and looked rearwards and as I followed her frightened gaze, the blunt nose of a nine-millimetre Makarov automatic, followed by its shadowy handler, emerged from behind the seats.

'Hi, Tempest; we meet again.'

I hadn't heard that voice for a long time and hoped I'd never hear it again. There was no-one I wanted to meet less tonight than Killer O-Kane.

CHAPTER THIRTEEN

LIGHT FILLED THE JEEP as a seven-hundredweight truck pulled in behind us.

'Mike, I'm sorry.' Cress's hands gripped the wheel. 'They were waiting behind the jeep when I got there. I....I thought they'd come with you.'

The pickup team; I should have warned her. Too late now and one thing I would never have foreseen was the identity of the "officer" leading them. Light reflecting off the Makarov just about matched the ice-coldness of his voice.

'Out slowly, both of you. Any tricks and she gets it first, Tempest.'

Two men came from the van behind; they were the same pair who'd shrink-wrapped Charlie Smallbright. One of them disappeared towards the darkened slip with a hand-held radio while the other took my forty-five and picked up the lead-thug just recovering at our feet. Killer motioned us inside and we filed in.

Second-thug was conscious again too, one eye blackening like a crater on the moon, the other fixed on me. Killer tossed him back his thirty-eight and laughed ominously. 'You've had a busy evening, Tempest. We found what you'd left of those other punks on the road back there and I don't think you've made any friends here either.' He glanced at second-thug massaging an eye blacker than my thoughts and nodded towards me. 'Go ahead.'

Second-thug needed no further prompting. He tried a leering smile that became a wince as the crinkles reached his eye, only adding power to the muzzle of his thirty-eight as he brought it down on the side of my face, splitting the cheek and sending white-hot pokers of agony searing brainwards. I sank back onto one of the weapons cases, temporarily dazed and only sensing the trickle of blood, Cress's soothing hand and my assailant raising his weaponry to even things on the other side.

'Hold it....' It was Killer and for a second I thought he'd been struck by a sliver of humanity. I should have known better; it wasn't mercy he wanted but silence. He was standing with his head cocked seawards, '....they're coming?'

Now everyone could hear them including even me above the sickening scream already filling my head: the rapidly advancing purr of eighty-five horse outboards.

The boatshed doors were pulled wide open. Outside a commando was talking on his radio. A minute later the inflatables arrived, at high speed this time with the same four crew of this morning. Leaving the thugs to guard us, Killer went to meet them and soon more boxes were being transferred straight to the truck quickly followed by those landed earlier. I glanced at Cress sitting beside me and took her hand in mine; something told me that minutes now would see death finding this remote corner of East Anglia. Second-thug sensed it too, raised his thirty-eight and pointed it towards us.

'What about them?'

Killer smiled.

'Two bodies down the road and two more here should make it look like some drug gang bustup.'

He raised the forty-five and fired twice.

IN THE CONFINES OF that shed the two cracks were ear-numbing enough to deaden even Cress's scream. I braced myself for the agony of red-hot lead in my guts and just as quickly realised it was the two thugs who were lying crumpled and twitching in the corner amid a fast-growing pool of ebbing lifeblood. Even those twitches stopped when Killer emptied the rest of the magazine into their skulls. The hammer clicked onto an empty chamber and the smoke-filled room was silent. Killer wiped the automatic and handed it to me.

'Take it, Tempest.' I did as ordered, feeling the grips and wishing there was just one more round in the mag. 'Now drop it.' Again I complied and Killer smiled. 'Just so the police can put the blame where it'll do most good.' He turned to the leader of the boat commandos. 'Are all the weapons ashore?'

The leader nodded. He was an impressive man with an educated Dublin accent and a good three inches height-advantage on Killer but his manner left no doubt who was in charge.

'All those allocated to the English group.'

'And the badge and star; where are they?'

'Safe on the ship.'

'Good. I'll join you later once the arms are delivered. Take these two with you; we'll deep-six them in northern waters later but not before I arrive.' He turned to me. 'That'll give you some time to sit and think about it, Tempest, just like I had all those years to sit and think about you.'

'Why the girl, Killer?' I forced myself to let go of Cress's hand. 'She's done nothing to you. You can let her go.'

Our captor shook his head.

'Not a chance; when you head for the bottom, Tempest, Miss Dysart here will be right alongside you.' He cocked his head and, with sub-machine guns at our backs, we were hustled outside and down to the waiting RIBs.

Small wavelets now lapped the foreshore while icy drizzle rode on the back of the gusting easterly wind. The prospect of an open-boat North Sea passage to oblivion was daunting enough but somehow worse without even the consolation of togetherness. Cress and I were quickly hustled into separate RIBs, the outboards roared to life and then we were idling astern, swinging round in the stream and feeling the shove as the coxswains opened the taps to full power and creamed us away.

We were heading seawards but where to then and to what?

AT THE CENTRAL CONSOL, the coxswain kept the throttle at full and the speed at max. Ten yards off to starboard, his opposite number in the other boat did the same. They could afford incaution now: we were miles from any habitation with every decibel of those throaty outboards swallowed by the muffling drizzle and blackness of a North Sea night. Even if someone on the salt marshes did see us, it would hardly matter: the boatshed's use had obviously ended for ever and this would be the last time Killer's RIBs would wash the slip with their tumbling wake.

Those twin wakes now stretched far astern as, with the ebbing tide, we clipped the fairway at a good thirty knots. On either side the desolate landscape widened away as the RIBs took the first heave of an incoming roller and we reached the sea.

It was still moderately calm but that state wouldn't be for long in this wind. Combined with the boat's passage and the hardening rain, it now had the cutting edge of frozen steel. I sat right in the bow, my back to the elements and face towards the two commandos, their own now protected by pulled down balaclavas. In the eerie red glow of the compass light it made them more sinister than ever.

From our relation to the swell, I estimated those compasses to be showing slightly east of north. We were heading up the North Sea and soon even the loom of the land was lost in darkness and rain and all I could see was the other boat and pure heaving ocean. Our slapping passage over the swell was kicking up sheets of spray that cascaded over the boat and into the faces of the commando crew. Finally, the number two took pity on his S.M.G. and lowered the muzzle. I noticed it was a Czechoslovakian *Skorpion*. I eyed the distance between us; could I spring quick enough to turn it back on them and gain control? Possibly but when I looked across to the other inflatable creaming along in looser formation just off our starboard quarter I knew I never would. The hood of Cress's anorak was just visible in the bows; there was no way I could try anything here and her there and they knew it. I huddled lower, alone with my thoughts, trying to drum up

heat and positive thought and finding neither as we sped to
our fate with stinging rain almost horizontal in the compass
light.

There remained one small hope: that Cress had managed
to contact Sir John Tracam. Had she really made contact? I'd
never even had the chance to ask. Even if she had, our predicament now was well outside of anything envisaged those
long hours ago but there was some comfort in the thought
that someone might know we were on the right side in spite of
all the evidence left at the point. It was only a straw but, combined with dog-tiredness and the motion of the boat, enough
to lull me into a blessed, if fitful, sleep.

IT WAS THE CHANGE in engine note that woke me. I sat up wip-
ing sticky salt from my eyes to find the rain stopped but the
ever-freshening wind kicking the sea into tumbling white-
flecked anger. They'd slowed down to stop us pounding.

I had no idea now of time or distance but it was still black
night with just the hostile white-caps and our own churning
wash breaking through the curtain of desolation. If the aching cold had been enough to numb the pistol-whipped side
of my face, it might have been worth it. As it was, the throb-
bing pain still won through, accentuating my feelings of utter
wretchedness. I glanced at the commando crew, intense and
unspeaking this far, but now showing a perceptible increase
in their forward vigilance that soon changed to recognition
and the exchange of relieved glances. I turned round and saw
a red and white light amongst bright deck clusters. We were
overhauling a ship from the port quarter. Another mile and
we were alongside.

She was about the size of a small coaster but with her
bridge well for'ard, two tripod masts sprouting a profusion
of aerials and between them, two squat funnels side by side.
Pitching only slightly in the moderate sea, her high bow would
sometimes plough into a rogue roller, sending sheets of spray
flying over the name I could now see clearly, etched in white
on her jet-black hull: MORRIGAN.

We edged in closer while figures appeared from the dull grey superstructure and dropped a Jacob's ladder way aft on the port quarter where freeboard was reduced to near sea-level. There was gear mounted on the stern and covered by a continuation of the upper deck, an open area ringed by safety netting and blue perimeter lights: a helideck.

The other boat ran in first and brought up expertly along-side the Jacob's ladder. Strong arms reached down and quickly pulled Cress aboard and then the RIB eased ahead to where lifting-gear already lay swung out. While she was hooking on and lifting aboard we were alongside and I too was jumping for the ladder and joining Cress on the deck.

She looked cold and forlorn but managed a brave smile as we fell into each other's arms. I took her pale face in my hands.

'Okay?'

She nodded.

'I think so, apart from being frozen stiff.' She looked up at the satellite domes and slowly turning radar. 'Mike, where are we? What's happening?'

I never got the chance to answer before crewmen were ushering us for'ard along the rolling deck. They all wore the same gear and woolly hats and the few spoken commands were given in a strange tongue that I only vaguely recognised as Irish Gaelic. Just below the bridge, a storm door opened and we were ushered over the high coaming, down two steep companionways and ever further for'ard to another heavy bulkhead door. A commando pulled it open and we were pushed inside.

No heat or comfort here, just bare metal frames and hull plates that curved sharply to a smaller bulkhead in the bows. We were in the bosun's store, a compartment filled with tins of paint, blocks, tackle, an outboard motor and coils of ropes. While one guard covered us with his Skorpion, two others took some short lengths of halyard and quickly lashed our hands behind us. Then we were pushed down onto some coils of warp, the door clanged shut and we were alone.

CHAPTER FOURTEEN

'MORRIGAN IS OBVIOUSLY A geophysical survey vessel; basically a floating computer that collects seismic data, probably for the oil industry.' With other thoughts too bad to contemplate, I'd chosen instead to answer Cress's original question.

'But also running arms for the I.R.A.' She twisted at her wrist-ropes. They were doubtless as tight as my own but at least it gave her something on which to vent some anger, 'I thought they were trying for peace in Ireland. How does the Irish Government allow an Irish ship to be used by terrorists?'

'They don't; my guess is that Ossianic Geophysical operate MORRIGAN under some flag of convenience but as long as the Union one flies over the north she'll effectively be a ship of war.' I twisted my back towards her. 'Let me have a go at your ropes.' Cress shuffled round until her back was to mine and I could feel the knots on her wrists. I blindly fumbled away getting nowhere and finally giving my numbed fingers a break. 'Sorry, Cress, it's useless; these knots feel like they were welded.'

She turned her head and I could feel the softness of her hair on my cheek. '

'Let me have a go, Mike; my nails are longer than yours.' She started digging away. 'But where on earth did Charlie Smallbright and his funfair come into all this?'

I'd been thinking about that myself.

'Charlie Smallbright was obviously smuggling drugs into England through the yard at Langsden Priory and then using his funfair to distribute them around the country. Somehow this group sussed him and decided it was also a good place to land arms. Doubtless, Charlie thought he was going to make a lot of money and instead got murdered for his pains.'

'But not before he'd kidnapped and murdered Lady Tracam. Where did that come into it?'

'Perhaps just to raise funds for these arms; an operation like this doesn't run on peanuts. The I.R.A. have financed themselves by extortion before and poor old Sir John did part with a cool six million. Or perhaps Charlie Smallbright did that one all on his own, caused too much agro too close to an operation and got murdered by his new bosses.'

'But your helicopter was blown up.'

'Good point; that had all the hallmarks of a terrorist job and there's another connection between this group and the funfair: Madame Lena LeVoy.'

Cress twisted round in surprise.

'The fortune teller; where on earth does she come into all this?'

'She's the one I saw flying out of Battersea with Killer O-Kane.'

'You mean the horrible man who seems to be leading this group?' Just a hint of suspicion crept into her voice? 'You two know each other don't you?'

There was the crash of water against the bow plates as MORRIGAN lifted to the building sea; it was time for more revelations.

'Yes, we met in Africa. He was ex-Viet Nam and your typical gung-ho warrior. When Nam ended he'd looked around for more agro and Africa seemed the best place to find it. We ended up flying for the same outfit'

'Doing what?'

'General operations for a diamond mining outfit in Angola.' It was time to change the subject and not hard to find a reason. 'How are you doing with those knots?'

She gave an exasperated sigh and slumped against me.

'It's no good, Mike; my nails are in ribbons and I haven't budged a thing.'

'Don't worry; rest a bit.' I held her fingers in mine as we supported each other, back to back. I thought of my sliver of hope. 'How about Sir John Tracam; did you get hold of him in the end?'

She shook her head and again I felt the brush of her hair.

No, I let you down there too, Mike. I got through to his secretary and explained we had important information and desperately needed to speak to him but she said he was still at his religious retreat and it would take time to contact him. Before she could get back to me there was a knock at the door and someone said it was the motel manager with a message from you. I was so sick with worry that I didn't even think and opened the door. Of course, it was those thugs from the fairground.' There was a catch of despair in her voice. 'I seem to have messed up things all round.'

Her head was turned and I turned mine to meet it until our cheeks touched and I felt the warmth of her skin on mine.

'It's neither your fault nor mine, Cress. We just got caught up in something too big.'

Outside the steel walls of our cell, there came another crash as a wave struck MORRIGAN's bow. It shook me from the depths of self pity. I looked desperately around and saw the outboard engine bracketed to a support stand on the for'ard bulkhead. How sharp was that prop?

I rolled off the warp coil and shuffled over until my back was to its shaft and my fingers were feeling the leading edge of a prop blade. I brought the cords into contact and rubbed away.

It was slow going because the blade wasn't that sharp and the cords were tough. I only had limited movement and, to make matters worse, every time I rubbed, my fingers banged on a starter battery alongside. Five minutes had me completely exasperated and when my fingers took another painful crack on the battery I swung round and gave it a vengeful kick. It went sliding across the steel deck plates to end on its side against the aft bulkhead, dribbling fluid.

Battery fluid; that stuff was corrosive. I shuffled over, lay on my side and held my bonds to the trickling cap. Cress watched with renewed hope.

'Will it burn them right through?'

The trickle stopped and I rolled back and joined her on the coil.

'No, but at least it will rot and weaken them. It's just a matter of giving it time.'

Above the rumble of the ship's main diesels there came a high-pitched whine followed by a thud from the stern. MOR-RIGAN had just landed a helicopter.

Perhaps time was something we no longer had.

FOOTSTEPS DREW CLOSER, HANDLES turned and then the heavy steel oblong of the bulkhead door swung open and in came Killer and two commandos.

'Just making sure you're nice and comfortable, Tempest.' His concern carried all the warmth of liquid oxygen.'

I felt Cress shudder beside me.

'You're enjoying this aren't you Killer?'

'Sure I'm enjoying it…,' he was still smiling but the psychopath in his nature was never far below the surface. He squatted down until his face was level with mine and I could see the hatred in his eyes. There was pain there too, a lot of pain from a lot of years, '….I had a decade and a half to savour this moment, Tempest.' His face came even closer. 'Can you imagine what fifteen years in a stinking cell is like with only the rats for company?'

My sympathy was with the rats but it was a time for discussion rather than provocation. While there was talk there was time and while there was time there was hope.

'It was your choice, O-Kane; all you had to do was tell.'

'And sign my own death warrant, you mean.' He stood up dismissively. 'Can you imagine how long I'd have stayed alive once they had that information? Less time than I'm giving you right now, Tempest. No, those jewels were my hold on life even if they did mean a beating and torture every day of every year. They kept me going....that and the thought of what I'd do to you if I ever got the chance.'

'But in the end they let you go, Killer. Why?'

He moved towards the door.

'Never you mind, Tempest. Just know I'm going to be rich and you're going to be dead.' Killer stepped over the coaming, paused and turned. 'Think about that, Tempest.' Then the door clanged shut and they were gone.

Cress was already thinking about it.

'Mike, what will we do?'

'Get out of here but these ropes need to rot a bit more yet.'

'Get out to where? We're on a ship in the middle of the North Sea in winter.'

'I know, but at least if we get our hands free we're not totally helpless.'

'How long have we got?'

'I've no idea but at least an hour or Killer would have finished us now.'

She needed something to take her mind off time and again she used questions.

'Mike, what happened in Angola? What was all that talk of jewels and imprisonment?'

'As I said, we were flying for a diamond mining outfit in the north. It was right at the end of Portuguese colonial rule and the country in turmoil. By that time even the freedom fighters had split into three opposing factions and when the Portuguese finally pulled out, insurrection turned to civil war and the country became a bloodbath.'

'So why did you stay?'

'Because there was work to be done: flying medevacs to the few remaining hospitals, lifting besieged families from the war zone.'

'And O-Kane was doing this work too?' She was right to sound incredulous. 'He didn't strike me as having one gram of humanity in his body.'

'Yes, but for ulterior reasons. Angola was a wealthy country and people were selling their souls for a safe passage. Killer saw opportunities and made the most of every one. His big chance came with the Ataydes.'

'Who were they?'

'Portuguese colonials going back generations and about the richest in the country. They owned diamond mines but that didn't help them much when they found their mansion encircled by rebels bent on retribution. We got orders to go and fly them out. We only had light helicopters and evacuees were told to bring only what they could carry in their pockets. Not hard to imagine what the Ataydes were bringing.'

'Diamonds?'

'More than that. For years they'd been collecting priceless jewellery from all over Europe, much of it from deposed royal houses. Their collection was reckoned to be worth millions and Killer couldn't wait to launch off.'

'And you were with him?'

'No, my aircraft had developed a mysterious fault. It took us twenty minutes to clear it and me to get after him but it was twenty minutes too long; halfway there I met him coming back. We talked on the radio and the news was bad: he said he'd got there too late, that the rebels had already overrun the place and murdered the family.'

'You didn't believe him?'

'No. In spite of him ordering me to turn back, I pressed on and found the Atayde mansion burning fiercely. That was odd in itself; the rebels always ransacked and looted but rarely burned. In fact, there wasn't a rebel in sight but there were bodies: a pile of them on the lawn. After a good recce, I landed.'

'And found....?'

'....the Ataydes all dead; mown down by small arms fire. But no rebels.'

'And no jewels?'

I shook my head.

'Nothing. When I got back I confronted Killer and had him searched but he was clean. He'd probably landed some-

where and buried them enroute. After failing to turn me back
he knew word would get around. It was the only thing he
could do.'

Cress shook her own head.

'But the bastard murdered a whole family. There must
have been something you could do?'

'Not much with law and order gone to hell. The Marxist
MPLA was winning anyway so I did the only wise thing and
got out.'

'And Killer O-Kane....?'

'True to character, he stayed and joined Colonel Callan's
mercenaries fighting a rearguard with the FNLA. It was a natural outlet for his psychopathic tendencies but he must also
have been planning to recover his loot.'

'But he didn't?'

'No; he'd backed the wrong side this time. Most of Callan's group was captured, put on trial and shot.'

'Why not O-Kane?'

'Because the Marxists knew all about the Atayde collection and wanted it for themselves. They also knew of my suspicions and realised Killer was the last link to getting it. So
they sentenced him to life instead and you know the rest.'

Cress sighed.

'Fifteen years of torture; any man would become obsessed
with revenge going through that.' The sympathy was only
momentary. 'But now he's out and going to be rich so presumably he escaped and got the jewels in the end. What were
the "badge and star" they said were aboard? '

Once again, I shook my head.

'I've no idea and I certainly don't think he escaped from
that place. Someone must have done a deal with the Angolan
government.'

'Who?'

'Easy. Did you notice that this crew all have pretty healthy
tans. What's the betting that *MORRIGAN*'s just completed
a contract in the Angolan offshore oilfields, been paid with

surplus soviet weaponry and had Killer O-Kane thrown in as part of the deal?'

She looked dubious.

'Why would they want him?'

I shrugged.

'Presumably for his killing skills. When it comes to that game, Killer is as good as his name. Believe me, he can teach even the best a few tricks: guerrilla warfare, unarmed combat, working knowledge of every type of weapon from sophisticated missiles to plain guns, knives and bombs.'

'Bombs,' I'd struck a nerve with Cress, 'you think he made the one in your helicopter?'

I nodded.

'No doubt about it; a work of love when he found I was the pilot.' I sighed. 'Fate dealt me a bad one putting me back in his crosshairs.'

'But it wasn't.'

I looked at Cress and saw she was crying.

'Wasn't what?'

'Fate; it was deliberate and I did it.'

'Go on.'

She sniffed back some tears.

'When we first met and you asked how I'd picked you, I said your name just came up. Well, that wasn't the whole truth: Charlie Smallbright gave me your name....told me to find you....said you were just the pilot for a job like this.'

'And we can both guess who gave it to him.'

'Killer O-Kane?'

'Had to be.'

Cress shook her head, sadly.

'I'm so sorry, Mike. You were set up for this and I was their tool.'

'Forget it, Cress; we both needed money and got ourselves in over our heads.' The lurch and crash of real water against the hull plates as MORRIGAN took another roller shook me back to the present. 'Time for another go at these ropes.'

I rolled off the coil towards the outboard and beavered again on the propblade. Blunt as it was, it was now hopefully cutting on weakened rope. I couldn't see a thing but somehow I could feel the blade biting and a few seconds later there was a definite slackening in my bonds. More frantic rubs and I felt them give completely and the blood drain agonisingly back into my hands. I was free. I leapt across to Cress and soon she too was rubbing bloodless wrists. We embraced in thankful triumph.

'Where now, Mike?'

'The door, but I need something to handle the guard.' I pulled a large one-ring spanner from its clips on the for'ard bulkhead. 'This'll do.' With my makeshift weapon ready in one hand, I applied a steady pressure to the bulkhead door lever with the other. It moved half an inch and jammed solid. 'Locked.'

'Oh no.' Cress sagged back against the steel in despair. 'If it's locked, why did they tie us up in the first place?'

'Because there must be another way out.' I turned towards the bow and the collision bulkhead. By regulation, it was devoid of doors but there was still access for'ard, a circular manhole cover, halfway up and secured by about twenty inch-and-a-half nuts. 'There's our bolthole,' I looked at my spanner-weapon, 'and this is what does the unbolting.' I put the spanner on the first nut and heaved.

Like the rest of MORRIGAN, the nuts were well painted but once the seal was broken it moved easily enough. I got it to where I could turn it by hand, left it and went for the rest. It was sweaty, vein-swelling work with the ship pitching more than ever beneath us. I turned to Cress over my shoulder.

'Try and find something to hold the door in case they come back.' She lifted the outboard off its bracket and jammed it between the deck and the downward-moving section of the handle. Not exactly impregnable but it would buy us time. The last nut gave and then I was hand-winding them off.

I handed them, one by one, to Cress to lay quietly on the deck; the last thing I wanted was these things clanging away like an alarm. I breathed again when I had twenty bare bolt-heads and not so much as a clink. Then I took the cover in both hands and pulled. It didn't move a hair's breadth; the paint was sealing it.

I pulled the dipstick from the outboard and used it to score away the enamel.

'Let's try again; give me a hand.' She took one side of the cover and we heaved away together. It started to move. 'For God's sake, don't drop it.' The solid steel cover felt like it weighed a ton and if we'd let that go rolling about the deck it would have sounded like Big Ben at midnight. We got it safely down. I went back to the yawning hole like Howard Carter for his first glimpse of King Tut's tomb and found the same impenetrable blackness.

No light but certainly smell and sound: the sickly aroma of bilge muck and rusting metal combining with the almost deafening sluice of water against the hull plates. As MOR-RIGAN gave another downward plunge, my heart went with her. We seemed to have slaved away to meet another dead-end. I stuck my head further in away from the compartment lights and slowly night vision returned and I picked out details.

Cress's voice came from outside.

'What can you see?'

'Chain.'

'Chain?'

'Yes, anchor chain. We've struck the cable locker.'

'With no way out?' She was stealing herself for another disappointment.

'I don't know; let me get in there and find out.' I squeezed through, ending up on all fours amidst the piled unyielding links. Two lengths climbed upwards to the port and starboard navel pipes but something else was climbing too: a vertical steel ladder like a pathway to heaven. 'Come on, Cress,' a second thought flicked by, 'but hand that spanner through first.' If we did reach the main deck I wanted more in my hand than muck and sweat.

Cress followed it through and we paused atop the cable pile with the sea crashing against the plates an inch away and the bow plunging and rearing like a rodeo steer. In the blackness of that cable locker it felt like the ante-room to hell but bliss compared to our condemned cell.

'What now, skipper?' She was close to me and, in spite of the thundering sea, whispering in the darkness.

'I'm going for a recce; you stay here.'

Rung by rusty rung I made my way up. At the top there was another cover, free-seated flat into the deck. I pushed gingerly upwards and it lifted just a crack. An icy shaft of blessed North Sea air came wafting down. I lifted the cover slightly more and brought my eyes level with the rim.

My worm's-eye view identified the focs'l with its capstans and mooring warps but, thankfully, no crew. I went back down to Cress.

'We're going up; me first, you follow. The focs'l deck itself is clear but it's in sight of the bridge and they're bound to have a watch up there.'

'So they'll see us?'

'Only if we hang around the hatch cover. As soon as you're through, head straight for the base of the superstructure; it's in their blind spot. Ready?'

She gave a nervous nod.

This time, I eased the cover right off and brought my head out after it. No-one on deck but above I could see the bridge windows and the red glow of nightlights inside. All it needed was for one of the watch to take a look for'ard and we were sunk. I hauled myself out, spanner in hand, knelt on the deck and helped Cress after me. She went straight under the bridge while I slid the cover back in place.

I joined her in the blind spot, shivering in the arctic air. The only immediate risk now was if a crewman came onto the focs'l; unlikely in these conditions but only until they went back to the boatswain's store and found us gone.

We stood there for a minute, the wind screaming in the rigging and the spray it brought aboard feeling like a million needles of ice on our exposed skin. I signalled to Cress to stay put, cautiously edged over to the high bulwark and looked out.

Below, the relentless waves thundered against MORRIG-AN's bow, only to be flung aside with each downward plunge like some constant duel between man's creation and the elements. Ahead and on all sides the North Sea stretched away in black, angry, forbidding desolation.

Where the hell did we go from here?

CHAPTER FIFTEEN

OUT OF THE FRYING pan and into the fire except a fire would have been a whole lot warmer.

I looked out across the rolling hostile waters and wondered how long we'd survive swimming: five minutes perhaps, ten at the most. Where were we anyway? Heading north, Killer had said, but the sky was too obscured for a star check. How far from land? Impossible to even guess; that same cloud prevented even the loom of a light penetrating the darkness.

But there was something there in the blackness. I peered deeper and fixed it just off the starboard bow, a small pinprick of light, stationary like a beacon of hope. I watched it for perhaps a minute before returning to the cold figure huddled below the wheelhouse.

'Cress, we've got to go over the side.'

She looked at me as though I was crazy and perhaps she wasn't far wrong.

'In there,' she nodded towards the foaming maelstrom, 'it'd be certain death.'

'No it wouldn't. There's a boat ahead. If we go over just as we pass we can hail them to pick us up.'

'How do you know? We might miss it by miles.' She was frightened and I didn't blame her.

'I'm sure we're overhauling it and the relative bearing's staying constant which means we'll pass very close. Can you swim?'

She nodded.

'Yes, but in that....'

I pulled her close.

Look, Cress, I'm not saying there isn't a risk but it's our only chance. Here, we've no chance at all. Any minute now and the balloon's going to go up and minutes will see us cornered and dead.'

'The helicopter....why don't we take that?....you could just fly us ashore.'

I shook my head.

'A nice thought but we'd never get off the deck. Even assuming we could get the thing ready undetected, it would take a minimum of two minutes to get both engines burning and turning. We wouldn't even get the first to ground idle before we had half the crew ramming SMGs down our throats.' I nodded towards the sea. 'In there's our only way.'

She had one last try.

'We could launch an inflatable or even push over a liferaft?'

'....and even fire a few flares for good measure just to make sure they don't miss us when they turn round to run us down.' I tried to neutralise my sarcasm by smoothing her cold cheek with my hand. 'Trust me, Cress.'

She raised her head and the appeal of those eyes mirrored the catch in her voice.

'Will you stay with me?'

I took her head in both hands and kissed her forehead.

'All the way...whichever we go.'

'All right.'

'Good girl.' I pulled up the hood of her anorak. 'We'll go to the stern; the deck's almost at sea level there and we can slip in with hardly a splash.'

We set off, me leading, her hand tight in mine. At the first ladder we climbed to the upper deck: less lighting and no gangway doors but strange canvas-covered shapes and plenty of shadows to give our stretched nerves a strumming.

Stalking along the deck, I constantly checked our light over my shoulder; was it really getting closer? Hard to tell but I was sure it was getting larger and clearer and still on a steady bearing. The faster and clearer the better because it was a race now before Killer and his crew found us gone and raised the alarm. I looked again at the light: definitely closer and giving the distinct impression now that it was stationary. Could it be just a buoy? I'd look pretty stupid if it was but lightbuoys usually flashed and this was a steady white light.

Finally, we reached the afterend of the upper deck where guardrails curved to separate it from the extension of the helideck. The Bolkow, blacker than the night sky and looking as stocky as a Sumo wrestler, sat with all four blades tied down and the skids shackled to the deck. The ship gave an extra heave as a rogue roller passed beneath and I looked from its creaming wind-spumed crest back to the helicopter. How tempting, as Cress suggested, to try for a runner at 115 warm, dry knots. Tempting and suicidal but there was another way the helicopter could help us.

I handed Cress the spanner.

'Here, you go down to the shelter of the cable deck below while I grab a couple of lifejackets from the chopper.' Down she went while I prayed they'd done the logical thing at sea and left the doors unlocked.

They had and as I eased open the pilot's, that indefinable aircraft cockpit smell came wafting out to remind me of a way of life seemingly lost in a week of nightmares. Well, we could all afford to lose ways of life as long as we didn't lose the main one. I grabbed Killer's lifejacket off his seat and the passenger one next to it, turned away and cannoned right into the figure behind me.

It was one of the commandos, as muscular and forbidding as the rest and probably detailed to check the helicopter in the rising sea. Whatever the reason, he was here now and my only weapon, the spanner, was one deck below. I had to act quick and instinctively brought my knee up into his crotch.

That's where it would have gone too if he hadn't sidestepped as smartly as a hyperactive monkey. Instead my knee glanced off his shin causing just enough pain to arouse his martial anger but at least taking his mind off immediate alarm. He was going to extract some personal vengeance for that kick before calling on any help from the others and he started by delivering a fistful of granite to my guts.

I doubled over in windless nauseating agony, a position perfect for him to land a second rattling piledriver to the side of my head. Amidst an explosion of cascading stars, I went down onto the steel plates and rolled into the deck-edge safety netting.

I lay there prostrate, getting my wind back and shaking the lights out of my scrambled brain. One refused to go and through the mists of semi-consciousness I realised it was our light, abeam the bow now and soon to be lost astern for ever. The commando reached across the netting to drag me back and I realised that in more ways than one I was going to miss the boat. As he grabbed my jacket, his head gave a sudden jar and just as quickly he let go.

He let himself go too, like a stick of wet spaghetti, into a silent heap on the deck leaving me looking at the divine spanner-wielding figure of Crestovana Dysart poised above him.

'Mike, are you all right?' She helped pull me to my shaky feet.

'Just about. That's another one I owe you, Cress.' I wanted to kiss her right then but there wasn't time. I scooped one of the lifejackets off the deck and stuck it over her head. The light was dead abeam now. 'Let's go, sweetheart.'

We scuttled down the ladder to the cable deck below but not before she'd taken one last look at the commando crumpled above us.

'Do you think I killed him?'

'Probably not but don't worry, just remember to hit harder next time. Come on.'

The cable deck was almost level with the waterline, built that way for launching the ship's seismic gear. The means to do that filled the cavern-like void: two massive three-kilometre drums of oil-filled seismic cable and, aft of them, the port and starboard airguns for firing underwater test shots. Other assorted gear stood lashed to the deck including a row of bulky objects on the centreline that I didn't even give a second glance as we raced for the starboard guardrail and looked for our light.

It was there, just beyond the creaming quarter-wave and travelling fast astern. Cress watched it in despair.

'We've missed it.'

'Not if we're quick.' I pulled the red tabs of our yellow life-jackets and, even as they hissed into life, climbed over the guardrail pulling her with me. A half-second's pause to give her a final kiss and the hull a good kick and then we were flying embraced straight into the tumbling ocean.

We hit, went under and just as quickly surfaced, every last gram of breath knocked out of us by the merciless sub-zero sea made even more confused by MORRIGAN's prop wash that kicked us far astern as she plunged on her way with no immediate signs of alarm.

MORRIGAN wasn't a problem any longer, the cold was. It was agonising, making me gasp and take down lungfuls of heaving seawater. I looked across to Cress; we'd stayed together but, eyes closed, she seemed in similar distress. I fought to control my breathing and presence of mind; the light - *our* light - where had it gone? From MORRIGAN's deck it had been clear enough but now, as we climbed and dropped with the rolling swell, my orientation seemed to be going the way of my bodily warmth. Then I heard the throaty roar of a starting diesel and on the next upward heave I saw it too, the white riding-light and vague outline of a large open boat.

'Start swimming,' I shook Cress from the lethargy that seemed about to engulf us both. She opened leaden eyes and I pointed, 'this way.'

We started off, hand in hand, two halves of a labouring breast-stroke, but it was too slow and, with renewed circulation, we let go and swam close but independently. That starting engine had me worried and even more so when the white light vanished to be replaced, lower down, by a bright green. Seconds later Cress voiced my horrible suspicions.

'Mike, they're moving....they're leaving us.'

From the stern of the boat, a frothing surge of propwash

followed almost immediately by a mounting bow-wave showed that Cress was right. Only fifty yards away, the object of all our endeavours was motoring away.

'HELP!' I stopped swimming and yelled with every last gasp my water-filled lungs could produce. Frantically, desperately, pleadingly. 'Heeeeellllp.!'

'Heeeelllp!' Cress was beside me now, her voice joining mine as we fought to regain our lost chance. Across the frothing waters the solitary green navlight was joined by a mocking white sternlight; our battle was as good as lost.

As if in parting signal, the hydrostatic lights of our own life-jackets flickered to life; about as illuminating as a match-flame in a cathedral but I spluttered across to Cress, 'Together....one last shout.'

'HEEELLLP!' Our last breath, our last hope.

Together, silently, we watched the white sternlight disappear. Any second now and the green would follow it and we'd be left alone to our futile miserable end. I took a couple of strokes towards Cress and, below the water, took her hand.

The green light didn't disappear though; it continued to shine and soon, to its right, it was joined by a red like the multi-coloured stare of some beautiful bug-eyed monster. I gripped Cress's hand in ecstasy; that combination meant only one thing:

'They've turned....they're coming back.'

We just floated there, treading water, waving our arms and cheering with new-found energy as the creaming bow plunged towards us. Then the engine note died and a sweeping searchlight beam came arcing over the water followed by a voice full of north country warmth.

'Bring'er beam on, dad....ah can see'um in't watter dead ahead.'

A minute later they were alongside and we were saved.

'Now, lad, what's thee doin' swimmin't oggin with'd lass on a night like this?'

He was a big man in his late sixties with the gnarled hands

and weather-beaten features typical of a life at sea. Cress and
I sat huddled in blankets while our sodden clothes steamed
before a bottle-gas heater just feet away. It was a fishing boat
to which we owed our salvation, virtually just a large open
boat that stank of cod and diesel and whose tiny for'ard cabin
in which we now thawed, was the only shelter aboard. Not
that we were complaining; she'd brought us life and no luxury
stateroom would ever be more appreciated.

They'd dragged us aboard like a prize catch, and while the
younger of the crew pulled off our lifejackets and outer clothing, the skipper had flashed up the heater, broken out the
blankets and brewed hot tea. Then we'd stumbled into the
oven-like fug and been left to complete our strip.

The North Sea in winter will cool anyone's ardour and
modesty was soon dissolved in the sheer joy of renewed life.
With our skivvies added to the sodden heap and us blanketed
round the fire like a couple of Indian braves, hot mugs in
hand, our saviour had returned with his question.

While I thought of an answer our skipper went to a bulkhead cupboard, produced a bottle of that sweet product of Ja-
maica, poured a good three fingers into our mugs and then
handed me the bottle itself. The first gulp went straight to
the spot with an afterglow that made lies of all those survival
books that tell you alcohol slows recovery. I passed it to Cress
and thought she was going to choke on her own first swig but
she took a second with impressive determination. If it was
designed to get me talking, it worked but the bottle was half-
empty before our kind host got his answer.

'Skipper....?'

'Hebditch....Tommy Hebditch.' He nodded towards the
stern. 'That's mi son Albert at 'elm.'

We couldn't see Albert because the hatchway was closed
but the throb of the diesel told us he was steering somewhere.
I only hoped it was away from MORRIGAN. I told him our
real names and we shook hands. He didn't show any immediate signs of recognition.

'Tommy, you probably won't believe this but we deliberately jumped from that ship you just passed.'

'Jumped....int'd freezin' oggin,' Skipper Tommy's face showed a mixture of bewilderment and reproval, 'ist thee crazy, lad?'

That good question again and many a psychiatrist might not have shaken their heads the way I did.

'I can't tell you why right now, Tommy, but, believe me when I say that if we hadn't we'd be as dead as if you'd never pulled us from the ogg...the sea.' I glanced at the marine VHF on the bulkhead. 'I'd be grateful too if you didn't tell anyone you'd picked us up.'

He scratched his stubbly chin.

'Sounds a rum'un to me, lad.'

Cress reached out and took one of the skipper's big rough hands.

'Tommy, no words can say how grateful we are for all you've done tonight. We owe you our lives,' the words were undeniably sincere but she was playing the helpless female to the hilt as well, 'but they're still in your hands. Please trust us.' She gave an extra squeeze of his hand; good girl, Cress.

Poor Tommy had taken a direct hit. He shook his grey close-cropped head.

'Ah guess thee knows what thee's doin', lass, and if thee don't wants me to tell no-un, that's hows it'll be.' He leaned closer and cupped her hand with his other big paw and his gruff voice was now touchingly tender. 'How's thee feelin' now?'

'A lot better...,' she gave her eyelids a token flicker, '....thanks to you.'

I hated to break into this touching little scene but I had a few practical questions of my own.

Where exactly are we headed, skipper?'

He dragged his attention back to mundane me.

'Home port, lad: Branscombe Bay, thirty miles and three hours west of here.'

The North Yorkshire coast; with Tommy's and Albert's

accents it couldn't be anywhere else. I couldn't hope to com-
pete with *femme-fatale* Cress but I tried the only other way I
knew to a man's heart.

'This is a *coble* isn't it, Tommy?' Even in my deep frozen state in the water, I'd noticed the curving, almost hump-
backed lines of this centuries-old stalwart of the northern
longshore fleets.

'Aye, she's a *cobble* alreet...,' every man is proud of his
boat and skipper Tommy even more so, '...belonged to mee
dad and as sturdy as the day she was built.'

I'd forgotten that Yorkshiremen alone pronounce it like
in *hobble* but Cress's words made up for it.

'Well, I think she's lovely, Tommy. What do you call
her?'

He beamed again.

'*VIKING SAGA*, lass.' Reluctantly, he let go of her hand.
'Now, if yeel excuse me arl go take a turn on't tiller while you
two younguns try an get some sleep.' He squeezed his bulk
through the hatchway, closed it behind him and we were
alone.

'What a lovely man.'

I nodded agreement.

'At least until he reads the morning paper and realises
he's trawled fugitives but you certainly seem to have won him
over to our side for now.' It was my turn to take her hand. 'Are
you really okay?'

'Mm; I'll probably never take another morning dip as long
as I live but at least I'm actually starting to feel parts of me
again.'

So was I and in parts I thought would never function again.
The warm cuddy and rum-fed sense of well-being had combined with the sheer relief at being alive to make our naked-
ness under the blankets more temptation than I could handle.
I looked Cress in the eye and the look back told me she felt
the same. I rolled towards her and she came unresisting into
my arms and in minutes that pitching, vibrating little cuddy
became a haven of love as I held her close and felt warm lips

that could so easily have been white and cold for ever.

'Mike...we shouldn't....Tommy and Albert?'

I put a finger to her lips.

'Sshh....they'll never know.'

They wouldn't either. As VIKING SAGA rose and fell beneath us and the wind shrieked its own song of rapture, for the first time that night I was grateful for the North Sea's fickle moods. The future was still full of questions but the ecstasy of the present would carry us through.

'MIKE? SHE SAID MY name questioningly and I knew she was checking if I was asleep.'

I wasn't; like her I was just lying in a haze of contentment.

Yeh...?'

She turned on her side towards me and ran soft fingers through my hair.

'I thought I'd never see another day, let alone know the joy of love again.'

I put my arm around her and pulled her close.

'It's an ill wind...and all that.'

A bad adage because just the thought of that ill wind brought some seriousness back into her expression.

'What are we going to do now, Mike? Shouldn't we be calling the coastguard or something and getting that ship stopped?'

I shook my head.

'Same old problem, Cress: with the trail of bodies we've left from London to Norfolk, the last thing the authorities are going to believe are stories from us about gunrunning survey ships. They've already unloaded all the arms back at the point so there'd be no evidence on board anyway.' I was dying for a cigarette but a North Sea ducking and a cuddy full of smoke was too much to ask in one night of any girl. Instead, I made her a promise. 'One thing we can do though is call Sir John Tracam again as soon as we're ashore and get him to pave the way for a meeting with the authorities.'

'Still after your reward, aren't you?' She was looking me straight in the eye but there was a smile in her tone.

I returned it.

'*Our* reward, Cress.' One decision I'd made back there was that if we ever came through this alive, any cake at the end would be split right down the middle. If anyone's earned a cut, it's you.'

'Thanks, Mike.' She squeezed my hand and brought her face to mine but this time our kisses were of love and com-mitment rather than undiluted passion. When we eventually came up for air I reached for Skipper Tommy's bottle, poured a shot into each of our mugs and raised mine in mock toast.

'God bless the VIKING SAGA; she can take as long as she wants to reach port; I'm content right here.'

She smiled but there was still concern in her face.

'So am I, Mike, but I still think the sooner we tell the authorities about MORRIGAN, the better.'

I put my arm back round her slender shoulders.

'Relax, Cress; there's plenty of time. By afternoon, she'll be up in the northern oilfields where one of the protection vessels can stop her. She can't get into much mischief before then.'

Worried eyes looked into mine.

'I'm not so sure.'

'How do you mean? What do you know?'

She turned in my arms.

'When you were up on the helideck getting the jackets and I was waiting for you on the deck below....'

'....the cable deck; what about it?'

'I saw something.'

'Saw what?'

'I'm not sure because I've never seen real ones....just pho-tos in magazines and on T.V.'

Patience had never been my strong point.

'Cress, *what*, for goodness sake?'

'Like I say, I'm not sure but, Mike....but I think they were mines.'

CHAPTER SIXTEEN

ONCE AGAIN THAT NIGHT, it was the change of engine note that woke me but, as I dragged myself to consciousness, the realisation of where I was and what I was doing there wasn't altogether unpleasant. The VIKING SAGA's cuddy was still as warm and snug as the girl in my arms.

It seemed hours ago that a combination of rum, exhaustion and contentment coupled with the boat's motion and vibration had driven us into blissful sleep. Now that vibration had changed and I was sliding out of Cress's sleepy embrace to the small brass-ringed scuttle above. Had MORRIGAN found us?

'Uh....what is it?' Cress was half-awake now, up on one elbow and vainly trying to wipe sleep from semi-focussed eyes.

'It's okay; we're just passing a breakwater: Branscombe I guess.' It was a guess because the light out there was only a shade brighter than total darkness. I struggled into my now-dry clothes and out into the cutting cold of VIKING SAGA's open well. It wasn't total deprivation because my cigarettes had also dried, the lighter still miraculously worked and in short order I was returning to unhealthy normality.

'Didst thee 'ave a good nap, lad?' Skipper Hebditch's concern carried just a sliver of innuendo enforced by a grinning wink to son Albert at the helm. We were idling into a small harbour whose stone walls gave way to picturesque little cottages of the same stone rising tier by tier around the sloping three sides. Lying at moorings in the still waters were a few private yachts and some more cobles of various size.

'Branscombe Bay?'

'Aye, lad, and always reet good it is to be back.' He seemed to read my mind. 'Missus'l 'ave fire lit and breakfast a cookin' by now; thee's welcome to join us.'

It was the best offer we were likely to get this cold morning.

'That's very kind of you, Mr Hebditch. We'd love to.'

Cress emerged from the cuddy. Her clothes were begging for a hot iron, her hair hung loose and uncombed and any last vestiges of makeup were long gone but she still looked a million dollars to me. As she snuggled wordlessly into my arms, we watched together as the sun's first ray tipped its wink above the eastern grey horizon.

'Dawn; I never thought we'd see another, Cress.'

'Nor me. Life's values have been seriously renewed.'

We just stood, savouring the moment, while the good crew of VIKING SAGA brought their sturdy vessel alongside the harbour wall and made fast. In the cottage on the slope, a light was already burning while smoke poured from its squat chimney and the smell of frying bacon and eggs came drifting down. Life is never all bad.

'THAT WAS THE BEST breakfast I've ever had.' I pushed my empty plate further into the large table around which we all sat in a living room that obviously served as kitchen, diner and lounge combined. In the grate a coalfire blazed cheerfully mirroring the beam from the large homely woman opposite.

'Thee's very welcome, Michael.' Mrs Hebditch refilled my bucket-sized teacup and then took Cress's hand with mother-like concern. 'Is thee alreet now, luv, after thee awful time las neet?'

'After that breakfast, Mrs Hebditch, I think I could tackle Niagara.' Cress put her other hand on top of our hostess's and I knew she was as touched as I was at this kind family's typical northern hospitality. 'You're wonderful; all of you.'

The Hebditches all beamed again and I knew there and then what I had to do.

'Tom, Albert,' the menfolk caught my serious tone and paused with their tea,' you saved our lives last night and if anyone deserves a full explanation, you do.' I glanced across at Cress and she nodded back. I took a deep breath and contin-

ued. 'This morning's newspaper will probably tell you about
the murder of some men in Norfolk last night; well, I killed
two of them.' Mrs Hebditch's other hand went to her mouth
and I'd got Tommy's and Albert's attention too. It wasn't the
sort of story they normally heard at their breakfast table but
I told them everything from the kidnapping to our pickup.
When I'd finished, I felt surprisingly relieved. Mrs Hebditch
looked at her husband.

Tommy didn't say anything immediately but got up, took
a large pipe, tobacco pouch and matches off the mantelpiece,
slowly filled the giant bowl and proceeded to flash up. When
the initial eruption had stabilized he leaned against the mantelpiece.

'That's an 'ell of a story, lad.'

'I know, but it's true.' I glanced again at Cress and then
back to the Hebditches. 'If you feel you should call the police, we'd understand; we don't want to incriminate you in
our mess.'

Tommy's Vesuvius had momentarily died and while he
did a quick relight I took the opportunity to flash up a smoke
of my own. The room was pretty well fugged by the time
Tommy spoke again.

'Naye, lad; thee's reet not to get rozzer's 'ands on thee 'till
thee's got summit sorted.'

God bless Tommy Hebditch and his good wife too who
gave Cress a lovely hug as much to say "there now, there's
nothing to worry about."

In fact there was still a lot to worry about and the sooner
I started neutralizing it, the better.

'Tommy, have you a telephone I could use?'

He'd taken the armchair by the fire now with his puffer
belching nicely. From beneath a pile of old magazines he produced an instrument straight from Alexander Bell's museum.

'Here, lad, dial thisselve but remember we's ex-directory
cause I don't want them suited wonders from't Food and Fish-
ery callin' with ev'ry new rule.'

'Even better, that way they can't get back to us.' Cress

dialled the number of Tracam Group in London from memory
and when they answered I gave my real name. That got me
straight through to Sir John's snooty secretary who told me he
was still away but had left strict instructions for me to be put
through if we called back. While the line buzzed and clicked
I lit up another cigarette and tried to catch up on fourteen
hours lost gasping. A well-modulated, urbane voice broke in,

'Tempest?'

'Speaking.'

'This is Sir John Tracam here, Tempest. I believe you have
information relating to the murder of my wife?' The slight
coolness was understandable, especially with his next words.
'You realise, of course, that you yourself are one of the leading
suspects. Six more murders since my dear wife's I understand.
Not exactly an upstanding citizen are you?'

I took another deep breath.

'I'm involved, yes, but innocent just the same. What I
need now is a meeting with you and some good lawyer to
prove it. Then I'll tell you who really did murder your wife.'

'Is this your sole concern: to see justice done?'

'No, I want the reward as well.'

There was a sigh at the other end.

'Ah yes, the two-hundred and fifty thousand pounds; a lot
of money, Tempest.'

He was right to be suspicious and I did feel sorry for the
old boy but I wasn't about to start eating crow for anyone.

'Yeh but not much use if you're dead which is how I've
almost been a half-dozen times these last few days. That six-
million you coughed up to the kidnappers was a lot of money
too and I know where it's gone. If we act quickly you might
get some back.'

There was a pause but only a short one because tycoons
like Sir John Tracam didn't get rich without being able to
think on their feet.

'All right, Tempest, we'd better get together. Where are
you?'

'In a village on the North Yorkshire coast.' That was as

much as he'd get in case Scotland Yard also had their ear to this call.

'Is Miss Dysart with you?'

'Yes.'

'Have you transport?'

'Have I transport....?' I was repeating the question but looking at dear old Tommy nodding his head, '....yes, I have transport.'

'Good; I'll get my secretary to make arrangements. She can call you direct; what's your number?'

'I'll call her in thirty minutes.' The police could put an address to a number before the phone was down and I didn't intend to involve the Hebditches. Before he had time to argue I had another more urgent request.

'Here's something you can do right now, Sir John. There's a ship called MORRIGAN steaming up the North Sea. She's carrying mines and you have to have her stopped and searched.'

'A ship.... Mines.... Stop and search...' patience obviously wasn't his strong point either, '. what has this got to do with me, Tempest? '

'A lot.... John. Believe it or not, that ship's very much involved in your wife's murder. '

There was another exasperated sigh.

'I have a lot of influential friends, Tempest, but I can't just pick up the phone and ask them to stop a ship. They'd think I'd lost my senses. '

'Well, try. MORRIGAN belongs to the I.R.A. and a good wodge of your six-million is tied up inside her. Get that ship if you ever want to see your money again. '

I probably hadn't gone to the top of his Christmas list but the point struck home.

'All right, Tempest, I'll see what I can do but you'd better not be making a fool of me. My secretary will be standing by for your call in thirty minutes. '

I hung up.

'So far, so good. '

Cress was optimistic.

'Thank goodness he spoke to you; he never even rang me back. With his influence and our story the police must realise we're innocent. '

'Perhaps, but let's see how much he really wields and how good a lawyer he produces. '

'And how much reward....' she smiled.

I grinned back.

'Yeh, that too. '

I smoked away the thirty minutes making plans. The Hebditches had an old van at our disposal with Albert as driver. Thirty minutes to the dot I phoned back Tracam's secretary to find out where it would have to take us.

'Leeds Airport. ' She was pompous but efficient with it. 'Sir John is still at his religious retreat in Scotland. I have made arrangements for you and Miss Dysart to fly to Glasgow on British Midland flight 294 leaving at five past three this afternoon. Separate tickets will be waiting at check-in in the name of Mr Smith and Miss Jones. A car will meet you at Glasgow. '

I told Cress the arrangements.

'Scotland! Why so far? '

'Because that's where he is and the remoter the better from our point of view. '

'Well, ' she stood up, 'whether by sea or air, we seem destined to visit the bonny highlands. At least things are finally turning right. '

I hoped so but somehow they still seemed all wrong.

WE MADE LEEDS WITH time to spare in spite of quick baths, the Hebditch's antiquated van, Albert's stolid driving and a stop to buy a morning paper. The latter made interesting reading.

SHOOTOUT IN RURAL NORFOLK proclaimed the headline and went on to describe the bodies of two men and the crashed Mercedes on the road to Langsden Priory. No mention of other bodies at the boathouse or Cress either though they did give a description of her jeep and its registration. Obviously the police hadn't yet discovered the mess at the point but doubtless they soon would. In the meantime they were still more than anxious to find one Michael Tempest, already wanted in connection with the Tracam kidnap case and the Hackney Fairground murders, who they were sure could help them with their enquiries. You bet he could but not yet.

I read the article twice but somehow it only increased my feeling of unease. I couldn't put my finger on it and put it down to apprehension at being recognised at the airport; the papers had repeated a fair but unflattering description that might just gel with some sharp-eyed official.

The first was the airline traffic girl. We checked in separately but made sure we got adjacent window seats and she handed over our boarding cards without so much as a bat of her long-lashed lids. I glanced sideways at the three police wandering various parts of the terminal and wondered if airports had always had this many or that I just hadn't noticed them in my old law-abiding days?

Thankfully, they didn't seem to be noticing me but, just the same, Cress and I kept our distance except in the seclusion of the carpark where we said our goodbyes to Albert. He went on his way, content with the promise of some day being able to tell this tale at his local. I'd make sure they had something to drink too when Tracam finally settled my debts.

Back in the terminal building, Cress and I made our separate ways to the departure gate. No passport check, of course, but the rest of the procedure was nerve-strumming enough for fugitives. With a calming cigarette and only minor palpations, I reached the gate just as they were boarding.

The traffic officer took his half of my boarding card but gave me a strange look as he did so. I scuttled down the airstair but a voice called me back.

'Just one minute, sir. '

I stopped, the sickness of despair seeming to enfold me. Should I run or try and brass it out? I turned slowly, the hairs on my neck standing up like barbed-wire.

'Yeh? '

'Please put that cigarette out, sir. This is a non-smoking flight. '

'Ah, sorry. ' I stubbed my cigarette in a tray and carried on to the waiting Fokker 50 with another ten years off my life.

The flight was two-thirds full but, with Cress beside me, I sat back and relaxed as we levelled at cruise altitude and the cheerful hosty started dishing the snacks. I was well into my needed coffee before I let worries reassert and whispered a question.

'You sure those were mines you saw on MORRIGAN's cable deck?'

Some of the gear on those seismic ships was pretty weird-looking stuff and I just needed to be sure I hadn't thrown old Tracam some duff gen.

'No, I'm not sure but I remember seeing TV pictures of mines in the Gulf war and those things looked just like them.There were just two of them though there seemed to be room for more' She just sipped her coffee and left the biscuits. 'What I don't understand is how they got things like that past British Customs?'

'The same way as the rest of the arms: by never clearing customs in the first place. There was no legal need to as long as they never officially touched British soil; MORRIGAN is simply a ship on passage.' I paused to help myself to her un-used biscuits. 'That's why they needed a secret drop for the arms. If she really is carrying a couple of mines as well, my guess is she'll drop them in the northern oilfields and con-tinue her merry way round Scotland to Ireland.'

I sat back and thought of the disruption and possible de-struction that even two mines loose in the North Sea would cause. Rigs and platforms might have to be evacuated and millions of pounds of production a day lost while the navy swept the area.

In trying to predict future events, my thoughts went nat-urally to that colourful young woman who made her living from it. Where was Madame LeVoy now? Where did the brazen Lena fit into this whole crazy picture? I thought too of the near past, specifically, my conversations of this morning and realised why they'd been troubling me. The jigsaw was coming together and the picture shocked even me.

I was still trying to slot in the most awkward bits when the *seatbelt* light flashed on and we began our descent into Glasgow. Time for another test: who would really be meeting us here? As we emerged into arrivals I saw the black uniform and peaked cap.

HE WORE GRIM FEATURES too and he had a card with my name on it but it wasn't a warrant; it said simply *Mr Smith* and he was Sir John Tracam's chauffeur.

That card turned out to be the limit of his welcome. Without a word he led us out to an all-black Range Rover. I'd been half-expecting a Rolls but a SUV was no doubt better for wheeling the winter Highlands. The pale afternoon sun still had a good two hours of burning when we crossed Erskine Bridge and picked up the road for Fort William and the Western Isles.

He drove fast and well but that formal cap had a strangely intimidating effect and we remained oddly silent in the back as the loveliness of Loch Lomond and surrounding Strathclyde flashed past at a steady seventy. In the end I broke the silence by asking the obvious question.

'Where actually are we going?'

'The monastery of Saint Fionn, sir, on the Isle of Braedon in the mouth of Loch Moeran. The drive will take about another three hours.' He had a deep Celtic burr that failed to disguise a forced courtesy and definite implication that further questions would be far from welcome.

A pity because I had no idea where Loch Moeran was and felt disinclined to ask. Instead I sat back with my thoughts and tried to enjoy a ride that by now was taking us through Glencoe. In the evening light its beauty was breathtaking but strangely sombre too as the ghosts of the glen's tragic past combined with my own troubled thoughts. With Ben Nevis astern, we skirted Fort William and had just passed shining Loch Lochy when we turned west.

The new road was anything but motorway and as it narrowed and curved between black fir-coated mountains, our speed slowed accordingly. We seemed to have spent this whole day travelling and I for one was getting pretty saddlesore and ready for a stretch. I leaned forward.

'Any chance of stopping for a break?'

The cap stayed rigidly on the road ahead.

'My orders are to bring you direct to the monastery, sir, but if it's refreshments you're after, then Sir John had a flask and sandwiches put in the car for your convenience.'

I leaned back into the open boot area. There was a canvas grip, presumably the chauffeur's, and, next to that, a wicker picnic hamper inside of which I found a flask of hot water, tea, coffee, sugar, milk and assorted plastic-bagged sandwiches. I mentally thanked Sir John and his obviously not-too-austere order and offered Cress first grabs but she shook her head so I ate and drank alone with the grandeur of the western highlands sliding by at extremes of speed as we climbed, crested and coasted the evermore undulating road to the isles.

I'd just finished my second coffee as the sun finally dipped behind the western headlands and we turned onto an even smaller road towards it. It was single track but well-surfaced and served by passing places for traffic we never met. To our left, sombre mountains rose steep into the enveloping blackness, their cragginess broken only by the white of the occasional burn gushing its way downward. On our right, the ground fell gently away to rocky outcrops and thick pine plantations between which we glimpsed the moon-fed glitter of open water. We were running down the south shore of a loch which I guessed must be the mysterious Moeran.

Not that I was feeling in a fit state to appreciate scenery; a few more miles had me clutching my stomach and my eyes screwed with pain.

'Mike, is something wrong?' Cress had taken hold of my hand.

'My guts..., I was gasping between gritted teeth,'....hurting like hell....probably something I've eaten.'

'Stop the car,' she was leaning forward and shaking the chauffeur's shoulder, 'Mike's not well.'

He pulled into the next passing place with an audible sigh. I sat with my head thrown back, eyes closed, breath surging like a blacksmith's bellows and Cress's cool hand on the side of my face.

'Bad?'

I nodded and opened my eyes.

'Let me get out....some fresh air....perhaps I can throw up.'

She helped me out and, doubled up, I staggered round the front of the big Rover. It was as far as I got; beneath its flooding headlights I collapsed to the rocky ground, retching and groaning. This was it.

CHAPTER SEVENTEEN

'MIKE.'

Cress tried to support me and, just as quickly, realised my weight was beyond her. Leaving me hanging from the front bumper, she wrenched open the driver's door.

'Don't just sit there; help me get him back into the car.'

He gave a grunt of annoyance, climbed out and came round. What he lacked in sense of emergency though, he made up in strength and his big hands under my armpits soon had me to my feet. A pity for him because his only reward was my elbow jammed fast and hard into his guts.

He went down, gasping like a venting whale but, before I could put my boot into the side of his skull, Cress came frantically between us.

'Mike....what on earth?.... have you gone crazy?' Her desperate hold on my arm took a second to free and that was all the time he needed to roll onto his side, reach into that smart tunic and pull out a nine-millimetre *broomhandled* Mauser.

A great weapon, the Mauser, but only a fool would carry one with the catch off safety and this man was no fool. Even as his right thumb pushed it to *fire* I was down on him grabbing that five-and-a-half inch barrel away from my own vulnerable chest. As I twisted it back there came an instant muffled crack between us followed by the pungent ominous odour of burnt cordite.

I stopped struggling, illogically wondering which of us had taken the slug and realising that he'd stopped struggling too and that his staring eyes were doing only that: staring. From the corner of his mouth, a trickle of fresh-pumped blood began to stain the collar of the white uniform shirt.

I pulled myself to my feet and went to Cress, standing over us with one hand to her mouth. Whether it was to stifle a scream or stop from throwing up, I wasn't sure but the words that came out were a mixture of both.

'Is he dead?'

The still-smoking muzzle of the Mauser rested by a burn hole near his right breast while the tunic around it became a spreading island of crimson. I did a token feel of non-existent pulse.

'He won't get any deader.'

'Oh, God.' She turned away and I had the feeling that the Mike Tempest Fan Club was fast losing its only member. 'That whole charade of feeling sick in the car was just to lure him out and kill him wasn't it?'

'No, I didn't intend to kill him and I wouldn't have if you hadn't grabbed my arm and given him time to pull that Mauser.'

A bit unfair, but I needed her off my back and her voice did tone down just a fraction.

'But I thought you'd had a brainstorm or something,' she wasn't subdued for long, 'and I might still be right. What's got into you? Why on earth did you do it?'

'I'll tell you later; right now we need to get rid of his body.'

It was a suggestion that met with limited appeal and she continued to stare at the still form before us.

'He's bald.'

People notice the most irrelevant things when they're in mild shock but she was right; his cap had rolled off and now moonlight glinted on the bare skin of his crown. I rolled him over with my foot and looked closer at the perfect bare circle in his otherwise bushy thatch.

'Not bald, Cress; it's been shaved like that.'

'A tonsure.' She leaned back against the Rover's grill, eyes closed and distracted fingers running through her hair. 'Oh God, Tempest, you've killed a monk from the monastery.'

The Mauser was still in his hand. I slid the catch to *safe* and pulled it free.

'Not exactly Vatican issue is it?'

She sighed.

'He's Sir John's chauffeur, for goodness sakes. After his wife's kidnapping it's only natural Sir John felt the need for some personal protection and armed his driver.' She shook her head like any sane person with the world going mad around them. 'And can you blame him with psychopaths like you on the loose. We've killed another man and you're not even telling me why.'

'Later,' I stuck the Mauser in my belt and indicated the bloody form spotlighted in the beaming headlights, 'first we need to chuck him in the trees out of sight.'

She rolled her eyes in disgust.

'This is getting worse....you can't just "chuck" a body....'

She was wrong there; you can and I did. What's more, she actually helped when she saw me struggling regardless, not with excesses of enthusiasm but the dastardly deed was done and then we were back in the Rover with me lighting a much-needed cigarette as I fired the horses.

'Where now?' She was biting her lip and pretty close to tears. A bit fearful too, I suspected, which was understandable considering the way I'd been thinning the population these last few days.

'Original destination: Saint Fionn's monastery.' I shoved the big car in gear and pulled away. Ahead and behind, moon-light bathed the cold empty road. Not a car, not a soul. Just as well.

'SIR JOHN TRACAM MIXED up in all this. Are you crazy?'

In the warmth of the Rover, cruising westward under the stars, I really was beginning to wonder myself but I was long past the point of compromise.

'Consider the facts, Cress. First, there were a couple of things said back in the Hebditch's cottage that didn't gel though I couldn't put my finger on them at the time. One was from you.'

'Me?'

'Yeh,' I wound down my window and flicked out another

butt, 'after I'd spoken to Tracam you said he never rang you back. Does that mean you left a number?'

'Of course; the motel's with our chalet extension; didn't I tell you?'

'No, and all the time I was wondering how the fairground crew followed us. They didn't; Tracam traced the number and directed his heavies straight to you.'

'You're just assuming that.' She wasn't convinced.

'Another question then: when you spoke to his secretary, did you give your name or mention my name?'

'No, definitely not. I just told her I had information relating to Lady Tracam's murder and needed to speak to Sir John personally.'

'Exactly, but he asked if you were with me. Okay, he knew my name from the papers but yours has never been mentioned so how did he know it?'

'From the police; they would have traced the jeep's registration to me.'

'Probably, but the papers hadn't mentioned that and the police wouldn't be likely to go discussing things in that detail even to the victim's husband. No, Tracam had got the word from the other side and probably MORRIGAN, seeing as all Smallbright's boys were curling their toes by midnight which is another point: he mentioned *six* murders since his wife's but at that time the newspapers knew nothing of the killings at the point. How did he?"

The wind caught her hair as she cracked the window for some Highland air.

'I still can't believe it's Sir John. His secretary, perhaps, in cahoots with the kidnappers. Why would a man murder his own wife and then offer a reward for information?'

'A lot of reasons,' I lit another cigarette with the dashboard lighter, 'and insurance is one of them. Most rich types these days carry kidnap insurance. I bet that quarter-million reward has actually been posted by some insurance company who've already dished up the ransome six.'

She ran another quick hand through her hair but there was a grain of acceptance in her voice.

'It's a pretty far-fetched story.'

'Sweetheart, in case you've forgotten, these whole last few days have been pretty far-fetched.'

'Okay....but why?'

'Try this one: old millionaire meets young woman and falls in love. Wife finds out and already suspects that hubby is supplying arms to the I.R.A. Wife threatens to blow whistle so hubby has her kidnapped and murdered and uses insurance payoff for big arms purchase.' I took another drag on my cigarette. 'Well?'

'Ridiculous.' She cracked her window another three inches just to show my filthy habits were on a par with judgement. 'Young women? Falling in love? Sir John at his age? You're just guessing.'

'Perhaps, but I'll go even further and give the young woman a name: Lena LeVoy.'

'The fortune-teller?' She still sounded incredulous but a little less mocking.

'Why not? It's her I saw Killer flying out of Battersea and the most unlikely people indulge in astrology; Raegan and the C.I.A. had been using them for years. Perhaps old Tracam indulged a bit too much.'

She thought about that one.

'So why didn't you mention all this before instead of having to kill that poor man back there?'

'Because I hadn't thought it out myself until the end of the flight. It was too late then and, anyway, I wanted you to act naturally in front of whoever met us until I found out where we were going.' The road ahead forked with the main drag swinging left round the mountain. I swung right onto an even smaller road signposted APPRAHANNOCK, slackening speed on the broken potholed surface as it wound parallel to the ever-widening loch. 'This mysterious Monastery of Saint Fionn is where the answer to this whole mess lies; I'm convinced of it.'

'The monastery! Sir John's religious retreat? You surely don't think they're involved in all this too?'

'Why not?' I stubbed my cigarette and snapped shut the ashtray lid. 'That driver's bald patch....tonsure or whatever you call it....remember how all those fit-looking commando types on the ship wore stupid woolly hats? How about if they were to cover up tonsures of their own?'

'You mean the ship and these arms shipments all run by a monastery?' She was facing me shaking her head, not wanting to believe it but prepared to be convinced.

I shrugged my shoulders.

'They wouldn't be the first religious order to fight the fight with more than a stack of bibles.'

She turned back and watched the track ahead but I knew she was giving my theory some serious thought. When she spoke again, it was almost to herself.

'You're going to have a hard job convincing the authorities on that one.'

I laughed.

'Which is why I'm not even going to try.'

This time her expression was pure frustration.

'You don't mean we're going to this....this monastery on another of your little Sexton Blake adventure trips?'

'Why do you think we're lurching down this excuse for a road instead of heading straight back to Fort William?' It was my turn to be intolerant. 'Strewth girl, the way I've been filling the morgues lately they're probably changing the charge sheet right now from murder to genocide. No, Cress, we're still on our own until we get more evidence.'

'Until we get the reward you mean.' She scrunched down in her seat, arms firmly folded, face dead ahead. 'Is it really worth it? And just how does the great detective propose to get this evidence?'

I didn't answer immediately because we were in Apprahannock now, gliding past white-painted houses and chalets that ran with the road right down to the water's edge. There was no other traffic and no people, just an eerie stillness hang-

ing over all. We stopped on the quayside, switched off the
engine and lights and looked out onto the still waters of Loch
Moeran.

About a quarter mile offshore, seemingly floating there in
the moonlight, was a small island, its western half dominated
by the rising might of a mediaeval castle. So this was Braedon
Isle and the Monastery of Saint Fionn. Somehow, I'd been
expecting the gentle lines of some benign house of worship,
not these castellated walls and circular turrets rising dark and
sinister against a twinkling backdrop of stars.

How deep was Loch Moeran? I'd no idea but it couldn't
be deeper than my spirits were sinking as I surveyed our goal.
Worming my way into Fionn's saintly embrace had never
promised to be easy but cracking that theological Alcatraz
seemed nigh on impossible.

I tried to think of an answer to Cress's question and instead sat there in silence.

CHAPTER EIGHTEEN

I LOOKED AROUND. WE were stopped on what was actually an old stone jetty that poked its bony finger straight at Braedon Isle. Alongside the jetty was a more modern concrete slipway. Presumably, a call on a mobile phone brought a monastery boat on request. Not an option for us. I refired the engine, made a low-revving one-eighty and slid out of Apprahannock the way we'd come.

'Now where?'

At least this was one I could answer.

'We backtrack down the road a mile or two, hide the car and then foot it back into the village in the morning.'

'And....?'

'....and do ourselves a recce.' It was as much as I could come up with for now.

She gave me one of those womanly looks in return but by now I was pulling off the road and easing the Rover between thick pines that fringed the loch. When I was sure it couldn't be seen from the road I switched off and sat back in the silence, the loch waters twinkling just yards away. There were worse settings.

'Coffee?' Cress had climbed in the back and brought out the remains of the onboard fayre, handing me a steaming cup and pouring one for herself.

'Thanks.' I reclined the seats and, with the dashboard clock showing ten, we attacked the remains of the sarnies as well. I turned on the radio. 'Let's see what the news says of us tonight.'

Not much to start with, the lead item, ironically enough, being about the good progress of the latest Northern Ireland peace talks. It was followed by news of the discovery of yet more bodies in Norfolk and how the police would now like to

talk to Miss Crestovana Dysart whose vehicle had been found
at the scene. I glanced across.

'Sorry, Cress, but you take second place to politics.'

She shrugged and smiled and went to switch off but I
grabbed her hand and stopped her as I caught a final late item.
It was the report from the Helensburgh District Court where
they'd been hearing the cases and fining several demonstrators
who, a month before in Glen Fruin, had stopped a road con-
voy bringing Trident nuclear warheads to the submarine base
at Faslane. By peaceful obstruction, they had only been able
to delay things for a couple of hours but the publicity on this
sensitive issue had been considerable. This had been the third
such action in as many months, led by the peace movement,
Trident Ploughshares. Many protesters had joined them from
other organisations such as Scottish CND and various religious groups including monks from the Brotherhood of Saint
Fionn at Braedon Isle.

'WELL, SURELY THIS KNOCKS your theory of the brotherhood's
involvement on the head. Far from supporting terrorist action, they seem to be on the side of the peacemongers.'

We were walking, hand in hand, along the sparkling
shore of Loch Moeran, moonlight reflecting off the still water
and a million stars above turning the clear sky into a lustrous
inverted bowl of tumbling brilliance. A good canopy under
which to sleep but, after the day's events and that last bomb-
shell on the radio, a prospect ever more elusive. Instead we
walked and talked but answers didn't come easily.

'I admit it seems contradictory but in some ways it's not.
If the brotherhood are supporting the Irish cause, then taking
action against Trident warheads and all things nuclear fits in.
Trident submarines cruising submerged through the Irish Sea
have sunk more than one local fishing boat and there's concern that the nuclear plant at Selafield is releasing contami-
nated material into the same waters. It's all a very contentious
issue over there so some of the brothers joining in demonstra-

tions is pretty logical.' I cast my mind back to the rest of the report. 'Who are this outfit "Trident Ploughshares?"'

'A peace movement dedicated to disarming the UK Trident nuclear weapons systems by non-violent means. In the past they've blockaded both Coulport where the warheads are stored and Faslane, the submarine base a few miles away on the Clyde. Two swimmers even managed to get into the base recently and spray-painted a nuclear submarine. The name comes from the Biblical prophecy, "beat swords into ploughshares". She squeezed my hand and brought us to a stop. 'Mike, are you sure you haven't got this all wrong. From what I can see, this brotherhood on Braedon Isle are supporting nothing but peace movements and there's nothing wrong with that.'

'Nothing at all but there's more to this than either of us can see and I still mean to find out what.' I glanced at her sideways. 'How come you know so much about this Trident disarming outfit, Miss Dysart?'

She gave a little chuckle.

'There's a lot you still don't know about me, Captain Tempest.' The chuckle faded to a smile. 'Actually, I have some experience of the nuclear disarmament movement, a cause I sincerely believe in. I even did a stint at the Greenham Common peace camp.'

I put my arm around her and gave a reassuring hug.

'Ban the bomb and all that stuff, heh. Well, there are certainly worse causes.' Talk of missiles and bombs though had reminded me of something else. 'That radio news didn't make any mention about mines in the North Sea oilfields did it.'

Cress shrugged as we started walking again.

'Perhaps MORRIGAN never dropped them after all. There were just two of them, after all. You heard that first news item: the peace talks in Northern Ireland are going well so why would the I.R.A. take any action at a critical time like this?'

'Perhaps the more militant elements don't want peace; just their singular goal of a united Ireland. Maybe they did drop those mines anyway and they just haven't hit anything or even been sighted yet.'

Cress put her arm around my waist.

'Who knows, but the significant thing was that there was no report either of MORRIGAN being stopped and searched which makes me inclined to think Sir John Tracam never took the action you requested.'

'Which, like I said, means he's involved somehow.'

She nodded.

'It certainly looks that way. He knew we wouldn't pose a problem any more after this evening when he got us safe inside Saint Fionn's.'

'Safe isn't the word I'd use. I wonder what he's thinking now we're not?'

'I don't know and I'd prefer to keep it that way.' She took my hand again and squeezed. 'Mike, why don't we forget this crazy idea of tomorrow's recce and just go straight to the police.'

'We've been through all that, Cress but one thing you can forget is the we; you're not coming.'

She stopped walking.

'Of course I am.'

'No you're not.' I looked out across the cold waters of the loch, Far away, on the northern shore, lights twinkled invitingly: presumably another small town well away from this evil corner of Caledonia. I pointed it out to Cress. 'Tomorrow you head for there and safety.'

But she shook her head firmly.

'No, if we're sharing the reward, we share the risks too. That was the agreement.'

'But things could get violent again, Cress, and you're a pacifist, you've just admitted it. I don't want to involve you against your principles.'

Once again she shook her head.

'My principles are that I'm against war and if we can stop those weapons we saw unloaded in Norfolk ever being used, then I'll feel I've made a contribution to peace.' She turned and faced me again. 'Mike, I'm coming with you.'

Those final words were almost whispered and as we stood there, hands held, I saw just the hint of misting in her eyes. I pulled her close and we kissed.

'Funny how things work out.' Her hair was soft between my fingers.

'Mm.' Her hand stroked the side of my face. 'In spite of all the mess we're in, Mike, I wouldn't want to be anywhere else right now.'

'Nor me.' We started walking back to the Rover but, in spite of our physical longing, in her I detected an underlying sadness. 'What's wrong, Cress.'

She smiled apologetically.

'Sorry, but I was thinking of my son, Robin. Here I am actually feeling emotions I haven't felt for years but he's at school, hearing dreadful things on the news about his mum and probably wondering if he'll ever see me again.'

I let go her hand and put my arm round her shoulders.

'When he learns the truth, he'll be very proud of you, believe me. You'll be together again soon.'

She smiled.

'I hope so because each other's all we've got.'

We were back at the Rover now. With the seats folded down and blankets spread we'd be comfortable enough. And warm too if my vibrations were telling me true. I opened the door.

'Not any more, Cress; not any more.'

'COFFEE, SKIPPER?'

I was stripped to the waist, sluicing myself down in dawn-cold water and as surprised at the voice behind me as the two steaming cups she was holding.

'You're a wonder; is it still hot?'

'Just about.' Her impish smile was as bright as the sun poking its first wink over the eastern horizon. 'I guess we kept things on the boil last night.'

We kissed again and then went and sat together on a rock by the water's edge. The coffee wasn't scalding but it warmed the innards and completed my contentment. I fished out my last cigarette and lit up.

'You should give up that unhealthy habit.'

'I will as soon as we've collected the reward; what's the book?' She'd been carrying some volume under her arm and now she laid it on her lap and gave it a tap.

'Road atlas; found it in the front.' She flipped it open to a marked page. 'I've found out where we are.'

'Great.' I slid alongside and followed Cress's torn nail across the page.

'Here's Loch Moeran with the village of Apprahannock right on its southern headland. This dot isn't named but it must be Braedon Isle.'

We were certainly up there, nudging the Hebrides north of Skye and a good seventy miles northwest of Fort William. I ran my own finger across the ten mile wide mouth of the loch to the small dot on its northern shore. 'This must be the town whose lights we saw in the distance last night.' I picked out the name. 'Lochmoerantown; makes sense.'

'And this is where we are right now.'

'About two miles from Apprahannock.' I stubbed my cigarette on the rock and buried the butt in the sand. 'Time to get walking.'

We made our way back to the Rover where I hauled out the chauffeur's canvas grip. Inside was a roll of black cloth which, when I pulled it out, turned out to be a monk's habit.

'So he was definitely one of the brothers.'

Cress shivered.

'Knowing he's dead back there makes it seem like a shroud; throw the horrible thing away.'

'Not yet,' I stuffed it back followed by the Mauser, swung the bag round my back and slid my arms through its handles.

'What are you doing?'

'Making it look like a backpack. This way, Apprahan-

nock will think I'm just an innocent rambler hiking my aimless way.'

'How about me?' she said it as much as a challenge as a
question, 'What do I carry?'

I held her hands before me.

'Sure I can't talk you out of it?'

'No.'

'Okay, sweetheart, grab the coats and look after the cash.'
The latter was wrinkled and waterstained and there wasn't
much anyway but she stuffed it into her pocket and off we
set.

We kept a little off the beaten track, between the trees,
ghosting our way through pockets of mist drifting in from
the silent loch. It would soon be dissipating as the rising sun
warmed and aired the highland earth but for now it was welcome extra cover. In the trees the birds were already singing
and Cress was happy.

'It's a good day to be alive, Mike.'

I nodded agreement and silently prayed I would keep us
that way.

'CHEERFUL LITTLE SPOT, ISN'T it?'

Cress was snuggling deeper into her anorak and I didn't
blame her, for Apprahannock was decidedly chilly in both
temperature and ambience.

We'd ambled in as the village stirred itself to sleepy life
but just what that life entailed was difficult to tell. Fishing
would have seemed logical but there were no boats whatso-
ever. Likewise, the state of the road probably put off most
tourists and those that made it would have found little cheer
when they got here. Not hard to see why; over all hung an
air of brooding malevolence and the ever-sinister presence of
Saint Fionn's monastery whose forbidding battlements were
already materialising from the mist like some surfacing monster.

I looked around.

'I could murder a good breakfast but I can't see a cafe, let alone hotel.'

'I can't even see people.'

Cress was right, the place was still strangely deserted. Without the diluting effect of others I felt disinclined to wander and instead steered us into the cover of a stone outhouse near the slipway.

If I'd hoped to find Saint Fionns less intimidating in the light of day I was doomed to disappointment. With its battlements rising from the misty waters, the castle seemed more like the lair of some demon king than a holy place of worship, a granite cliff of awesome invincibility. From the highest turret, a flagless pole rose amidst arrays of historically incongruous aerials.

'The brothers obviously don't believe in total isolation from the mortal world. I wonder what goes on round the other side?'

It was impossible to see because on the isle's eastern end a thick plantation of pines made pleasing contrast to the castle's greyness but effectively hid everything on that northern side. There was sound though, the unmistakable rumble of low-revving diesels and soon, from behind the trees, a small stocky vessel appeared idling slowly astern, a ramp lifting at the for'ard end of her all-black hull.

'What's that?' Cress was gripping my arm.

'A tank landing craft. They must have a slipway on the other side.'

Clear of the point, the L.C.T.'s engines went ahead in a welter of propwash and then she was swinging round until her blunt bows pointed straight at the slipway yards from our hide. Ahead of her wheelhouse, we could see a small jeep, not unlike Cress's except this was painted all black like its big Rover brother.

'So that's how they get their vehicles to the island.'

Cress nodded.

'Saves them having to offload supplies into boats.'

'And keeps things secret too. A good way if you can afford

it which doesn't seem to be a problem with this order; not exactly rattling their begging bowls, are they?'

'Perhaps they have a generous benefactor.' She glanced towards me questioningly. 'Sir John Tracam?'

'Whoever it is likes all-black. Remember the Bolkow and MORRIGAN's hull? That was Ossianic Geophysical's paint scheme too.'

She nodded

'I wonder where they are now: the ship, the helicopter, Killer O-Kane?'

'Who knows.' The present scene was intriguing enough. The L.C.T. was at the slip now, gliding in and lowering her ramp in one smooth operation. Black-habited figures appeared on deck, cowls up and faces invisible. An aura of mystery and secret menace seemed to float with them on the dawn mist. I felt Cress's hand slip into mine.

'Strewth, they're creepy.'

'Intentionally so.' I watched as the jeep drove ashore followed by two brothers from the deck. There was an animated conversation on the quayside but the cowls hid more than their faces and I didn't hear a word. I could guess the subject though. 'Looks like they've lost something.'

Cress allowed herself a smile.

'Well, they won't find it here.' Evidently they thought so too because the jeep drove off down the inland road while the two on foot moved into the village. With the long habits hiding their feet, they moved with an almost ghostlike glide.

They weren't the only things moving now: real villagers were finally appearing and making a definite effort to avoid the black brothers. That didn't stop some being questioned by the monks and their responses being a unanimous shaking of heads. I was as glad as the brothers seemed frustrated. They moved on but the glances the villagers gave them showed the black order were anything but welcome in Apprahannock.

It was time for us to move too. The small store and post office across the street had just opened its shutters. If it was like any other in the country it would also double as local gossip control.

'Come on Cress; we need food, cigarettes and information.'

Inside, everything was small including the old lady who stood arranging shelves behind the counter. A jangling doorbell announced our entry causing her to whip round in near-panic clutching a small gold cross at her neck.

'Good morning; we just need supplies.' Cress's voice had gone some way to calming the old girl but she still made a tactful move behind the wire mesh of the Post Office.

While Cress collected food from the shelves I went into full-rambler mode.

'Can you tell us where we could find somewhere to stay round here; were on a walking tour.'

'Yeel find nae accommodation in Apprahannock.' Her voice had a quaver in it and just to make sure I was under no delusions she added, 'Naebiddy evur stops in Apprahannock.'

I could believe that but I nodded in the direction of Braedon Isle.

'We study old religious orders. What can you tell me about the monastery out there?'

'Saint Fionn's?' She leaned towards me with darting eyes and panic in her voice. 'Take my advice, mon, and forget it. Ye and the lassie just get out of Apprahannock the way ye come and be quick aboot it.'

I quit the charade.

'Why are you all so scared here? What does the brotherhood do?'

She never got to answer because the doorbell jangled again and once more she reached for her cross. With good reason this time because two black-shrouded figures darkened the doorway. They'd come, we were cornered and the Mauser was twenty porridge packets away.

CHAPTER NINETEEN

THEY CLOSED THE DOOR behind them and the bell clanged again but this time like the changes of doom. Even in the shop they kept their cowls well forward and hands folded inside big sleeves. I wondered what else they'd got hidden there and wished more than ever I'd kept my own hardware nearer to hand.

Cress must have read my thoughts; she was digging deep inside the bag and I knew it wasn't for her purse. I hoped she could throw straight. The two monks wandered amongst the shelves, seemingly browsing but sizing us up and listening to every word.

Surprisingly, it was the old postmistress who broke the silence. She turned back to me.

'Ye took the wrong road, sur,' she said in a trembling voice, 'Lochmoerantown is round the loch on the other side.'

'Thanks.' The monks were on the other side of the central shelf now. I went over to Cress and almost shoved her out the door.

'Mike, I haven't even paid for these goods.'

'Don't worry, I'll send her a cheque; let's get clear of this place while we can.' I took her hand again and half-pulled her along the road. Cress handed me the bag.

'Phew, I thought we'd had it that time. Why did they let us leave anyway? Presumably it was us they were looking for.'

I pulled the Mauser out of the bag and jammed it into my belt.

'Yeh, but with what the old girl said, they couldn't be sure. There's definitely strange things going on in Apprahannock but the last thing those monks want is suspicion reaching the outside world.' I glanced back along the road but there were no black brothers on our trail. Nevertheless, we kept the pace going until we'd cleared the village and could leave the road for the shelter of the lochside trees. A quarter-mile along the shore we found a rock projecting out into the water and sank down on it exhausted. I needed to know if one phase of the operation had been successful.

'Did you get the cigarettes?'

'Yes.' She pulled out a packet.

'Good.' I shook one out and gratefully flashed to life. 'Much more of this and I'll be needing them by the carton.'

'You're not the only one.' To my astonishment she helped herself to a cigarette, pulled mine across and lit up. 'I tell you, Mike, those monks back there really gave me the shakes. Those black habits and hoods make them look so sinister and....evil.'

'And it works; you can see how they've got the villagers intimidated.'

'How?'

'Who knows: coercion, threats, perhaps even hostages.'

'I hope the old postmistress is all right.'

'So do I. I wonder why she gave us directions for Lochmoerantown?'

'Like you said: to throw those monks off our backs.'

'I know, but I'm thinking she was trying to tell us something else. Remember, I'd just told her we wanted information on the order. Perhaps Lochmoerantown is where we'll find it.'

Cress looked out across the loch to where the morning sun reflected off white buildings far on the other side.

'Let's go find out; nothing to lose and better than staying here.'

I agreed. We stubbed our cigarettes and set off again along the shore towards the hidden Rover. I was glad she'd suggested going to Lochmoerantown. I didn't tell her why but in the back of my mind was a very good reason of my own.

•   •   •

'CERTAINLY A BRIGHTER SPOT than Apprahannock.' Cress was watching the white-painted cottages of Lochmoerantown glide by.

'Not difficult.' After the village we'd just left, this small town was almost bustling. I pulled into a parking slot looking out onto the loch, pleased to see real people walking, cars driving and boats moored to the quay. I took the Mauser from its position of readiness down by my feet and slipped it into the map compartment. 'I'm glad we didn't need that.'

Thirty miles back we'd passed the site of the chauffeur's body and Cress had given a little shudder and me a sigh of relief that it hadn't been found but until we rounded the loch and started heading west again I'd worried we'd meet the other monk jeep coming back. The fact that we hadn't probably meant it was retracing our complete route back to Glasgow. Good luck to them and more time for us but Cress was still worried.

'What if this vehicle's been reported stolen and we get spotted by police?'

I shook my head

'A risk we'll have to take but I'm sure it hasn't. I've a feeling the last thing the brothers want is contact with authority.'

'Well, that makes two of us. Where do we go from here?'

'You to the library, if Lochmoerantown's got one. It'll be a good start for finding out anything you can about the order.'

'Okay.' She looked at me suspiciously. 'Where are you going?'

'To check out a little plan of my own.' I nodded towards a small coffeehouse nestling by the quay. 'We'll meet in there in an hour and swap progress.'

We went our separate ways, me heading further downquay where most of the fishing boats lay at moorings and crews sat mending nets and passing the day. It didn't take long for my genuine love of boats to turn suspicion into friendship. They showed me their boats: broad-beamed luggers mainly owned by business types from the city who felt the odd Saturday hauling the net made them harder in the boardroom. This little be-smocked group though were the genuine article and the last bastion of real fishermen who knew no other life. I thought of Tommy Hebditch at Branscombe and what a salt-of-the-earth bunch they were.

It took an hour of pleasant banter but eventually I made my play, closed a deal, handed over a waterstained fifty and joined Cress back at the cafe. She was already finishing her first cup.

'Sorry I'm late'

'That's okay. I ordered us breakfast. Bacon and eggs sound okay?'

'Perfect.' I poured myself a coffee from the pot. 'Tell me what you found out.'

'That the library was closed today, so I did a rerun of this morning and went to the post office.'

'And....?'

'....and they didn't know much about the Brotherhood of Saint Fionn either but knew someone who probably did.'

'Who?'

'Pastor James MacFarn. He's a retired priest and a student of old religious orders, local history and hagiography.'

'Hagi-what?'

'Hagiography; it's the study of saints.'

'He won't find many to study round here.' The girl brought our breakfasts and we dug in. 'Sounds our man though. Any contact?'

She nodded.

'The post office gave me his number and I rang it straight away. He sounds a lovely old man and invited us to his house for a chat in about an hour.'

'Great.' I pushed away my empty plate, lit a cigarette and poured Cress another coffee. 'You've done well, Cress.'

'I hope so' She warmed her hands around the cup. 'How about you; what did you get scheming?'

'I'll tell you later. Did you find anything else out at all?'

'Only one thing.' Her face clouded slightly.

'What?

'Well, I got the post office to also give me the number of the one at Apprahannock; I wanted to ring the old postmis-tress there and promise to send the money for the shopping.'

'And....?'

'I rang the number but a strange man answered and said there was no old postmistress working there and never had been. Mike, do you think.....?'

I did, and the sooner we sorted out the Brothers of Brae-don Isle, the healthier this beautiful part of the world would be.

CHAPTER TWENTY

PASTOR MACFARN'S HOME WAS a smallish white bungalow on the edge of town, slightly elevated and with uninterrupted views of Loch Moeran and the open sea. A buxom house-keeper answered the door and showed us into a room sun-lit and bright in spite of wall-to-wall books. In one corner, a small white-haired man spun his wheelchair and came to meet us with a ready smile.

'You must be the young lady who called me and you are....?'

'Tempest, Mike Tempest.' Somehow, this was another man I didn't feel inclined to lie to.

If he recognised the name he didn't show it.

'And ye need information on the brotherhood across the loch?' His Scottish accent was smoothed by education and kindness.

I sat down with Cress on the sofa facing.

'Anything you can tell us, Pastor.'

'Which isn't much, I'm afraid.' He glanced over his shoulder towards the unseen Braedon Isle. 'The Saint Fionns are, to paraphrase our late Sir Winston, a mystery wrapped in an enigma.'

'How old is the brotherhood?'

'Very old. There is documentary evidence going back to the eighth century; the beginnings of Irish history as we know it. The period when, according to legend, one Cormac Ma-cArt was High King of Erin.'

'Irish?' I glanced at Cress and her eyebrows raised with mine.

'Oh yes, their whole history is Irish. Ireland is where the order started, flourished and became a thorn in the British side in the mid-sixteen-hundreds when Oliver Cromwell was battering Ireland to its knees.'

Cress helped herself to a cup of coffee brought in by the housekeeper.

'Not a particularly gladdening chapter in our history, I understand?'

Pastor MacFarn shook his head sadly.

'No, it was a time of terrible cruelty and oppression and the Saint Fionns were not prepared to take it passively. Apparently they had always had a militant streak but with the coming of the Ironsides they took a more aggressive role under the cover of religious order.'

'Such as?'

'Oh, righting wrongs here and punishing the guilty there. Murder and arson by any other name but always in the cause of defending the weak. Incidentally, it was at this time that they adopted Fionn as their saint.'

'Who was he?'

'Not a saint at all, I'm afraid, which rather offends hagiographic propriety. Fionn MacCumhaill, or Finn MacCool as he's more popularly known, was a leading character in the Fenian or Ossianic cycle of early Irish mythology.'

'Ossianic?' He'd pronounced it O-sheenic but the word still struck an immediate nerve with us both.

'Yes. Fenian was the name eventually adopted by the republican movement but the Ossianic cycle were a sort of splinter group of the original mythical Fenians. Fionn was the leader of the Fianna, the bodyguard of the High Kings, and one of the great heroes of ancient Eireann. This bodyguard aspect must have appealed to the brothers when they were looking for a saint. Whatever, it soon became one to be feared by Cromwell's administration.'

I poured myself another coffee.

'A sort of Knights Templar of Ireland?'

The old man nodded.

'Yes, very much so; part religious order, part secret society. In addition to strict religious observance, incumbents to the Saint Fionns were expected to show physical prowess and maintain martial skill. It's a tradition I believe they maintain to this day.'

'They certainly do but what about after the seventeenth century; where did they go then?'

'From strength to strength by all accounts,' our host took a sip of his own coffee, 'but still in their home country. By the time of the Easter Rebellion in 1916 they'd established several monasteries throughout Ireland. British Intelligence were always sure they were acting as rebel training depots, armouries and sanctuaries but totally impotent to do anything about it. The brotherhood was literally on sacred ground.'

Cress leaned forward.

'So why did they leave Ireland? When the Free State became a reality in 1922, they'd got what they wanted.'

Pastor MacFarn nodded and smiled.

'Yes, but remember that British withdrawal was followed almost immediately by civil war in Ireland and for once the Saint Fionns had backed the wrong side. When peace returned and the *Dail* finally agreed to accept the terms of the original treaty, they made it clear they wanted nothing to do with an order so opposed to partition. The brothers took the hint, closed down their Irish monasteries, bought the castle on Braedon Isle and continued here. We weren't happy of course; most of Ulster remained part of the United Kingdom and *Sinn Fein* were still sworn to drive us out. The British Government suspected the new monastery might be just a base on mainland Britain from which to continue that fight.'

And they weren't far wrong, I thought, but didn't say.

'Then why on earth did they let them come?'

'They had very little choice. Ireland at that time had dominion status and the brothers were all British subjects. I believe they were kept under surveillance for a while but fears proved groundless and eventually they were allowed to pursue the more benign aspects of their calling.'

'But these are dangerous times again, Pastor. Surely the

security forces would be well advised to at least give them a look?'

Our host shrugged his shoulders.

'But why, with all the good work the brotherhood do for many causes? Oh, I know this last year they've been a thorn in the side of the authorities by joining in these actions to stop Trident warheads coming into Scotland but the demonstrations have all been totally non-violent. My own theory is that the brotherhood, by nature of their history, need some cause to fight and this just provides a benign way of following their traditions.'

'Haven't the authorities taken any action against them for that?'

Pastor MacFarn smiled.

'Nothing other than a few fines and slapped wrists. No, I'm afraid that if our government started targeting groups like the Saint Fionns, they would soon face accusations of religious persecution. Besides, the order are not without political power of their own; they have their own friends in high places.'

'Like Sir John Tracam, you mean. I understand he is one of their chief benefactors?'

'Sir John Tracam, their benefactor?' The old pastor seemed faintly amused, not to say a little mocking. 'No, I'm afraid you're wide of the mark in that assessment, Mr Tempest. Sir John is far more than just a benefactor to Saint Fionns; he was brought up by them and is now their honorary abbot.'

I glanced across at Cress; neither of us was ready for that one.

'How come?'

Everyone likes to shock and Pastor MacFarn was no exception. He gave another little smile.

'What you obviously don't know is that Sir John Tracam was born in Ireland. His parents were humble people but deeply involved in local politics.'

'Republicans?'

'More separatist than republican and definitely not rebels.

Unfortunately, once insurrection was in full swing, nobody bothered to draw too fine a line between the two. In 1921 they held a meeting heavily attended by the I.R.A. The Black and Tans got word of it and went along to make arrests.'

'Black and Tans,' Cress leaned forward, 'they were our hit squads weren't they?'

The pastor nodded.

'Yes, auxiliary police with a reputation for ruthlessness that has left a mark on Ireland to this day. Inevitably, at the meeting, shooting broke out and both parents were killed.'

'Which must have left the son pretty bitter?' I was beginning to see some meaning to all this.

'Yes, of course. The boy had no other family so he was taken in by the Saint Fionns and given a good education which he justified by going on to university and graduating in engineering. Shortly after, probably with brotherhood money, he set up his own construction business, which became the conglomerate we know today.'

'Making lots of money for him and the brotherhood.'

'Doubtless, though I believe diversification into other fields has caused the odd cash crisis of late.'

'You're as well versed in corporate finance as you are in history, pastor.'

The old man smiled.

'I supplement my small pension by playing the stock market so reading the financial page is a daily necessity.' He tapped the wheels of his chair. 'About the only excitement I do get, these days.'

'Then you can probably tell me if one of the Tracam Group diversifications has been into the field of offshore survey?'

Pastor MacFarn nodded.

'Indeed, yes. With just one ship, I believe, under the name of Ossianic Geophysical. Bearing in mind his background, a clever play on words, don't you think?'

I agreed.

'How about MORRIGAN; does that name have any significance in Irish mythology?'

He seemed pleased to be away from financial futures and back into historical fact.

'Indeed it does: Morrigan was the major goddess of war, death and destruction. She took many forms but her favourite was as a crow or a raven.'

Black birds; I thought of another with that colour scheme and wondered where its pilot was right now. It was time to go; I nodded to Cress and we stood up.

'Pastor MacFarn, you've given us a wealth of useful information more vital than you can imagine.' We shook hands and turned to leave before I remembered something else, something we'd heard on *MORRIGAN*. 'One final thing, Pastor: does a star and badge mean anything to you?'

'In the context of Ireland?'

'Yes.'

'Then, what you are doubtless talking about are the Irish Crown Jewels, stolen from Dublin Castle in 1907.'

I SAT DOWN AGAIN.

'The what?'

'The Regalia of the Royal Order of St Patrick, to give the insignia their correct name. William IV had presented the Star and Badge of the Order in 1830.'

'But later stolen, you say?'

'Yes, and from Dublin Castle, then one of the most fortified buildings in the kingdom.'

'By who?'

MacFarn shook his head, smiling.

'Ah, there's the mystery or should I say, secret. There were deep suspicions against some in high office but no charges were ever brought to bear.'

'And the jewels were never found?'

'Never, in spite of a thousand pounds reward.'

I glanced at Cress and she raised her eyebrows and leaned closer towards our host.

'How were they stolen, Pastor MacFarn?'

The old man settled deeper into his wheelchair and placed

his fingertips together as he must have done a thousand times in the pulpit of his kirk.

'It was just four days before a state visit by King Edward VII. The insignia were in the charge of Sir Arthur Vicars, the Ulster King of Arms, Chief Herald of Ireland and registrar and knight attendant to the Order of Saint Patrick. He kept them in a safe in the library of the Bedford Tower, then the Office of Arms.'

'You mean they weren't in a strongroom?' I interrupted. 'How much were these insignia worth?'

'The official valuation was thirteen and a half thousand pounds which would be over a million in today's money, but that was just the face value of the stones. Allowing for their historical interest and the beautiful pieces of workmanship they represented, their true value would be at least ten times that amount. Apart from the Star and Badge, also stolen were five collars of the Companions of the Order plus some personal jewellery belonging to the Vicars family. Of course, they should have been in a strongroom and one had actually been built on the same floor. Unfortunately, it was found that the safe was too big to go through the door so it stayed in the library which, incidentally, was often used as a public waiting area. Vicars, who by all accounts was a fussy pedantic sort of person, had been pushing for a new safe that would fit but, by the time of the robbery, had been unable to get the treasury to approve the funds.'

'Unbelievable.' Cress was shaking her head. 'The thieves seem to have had bureaucracy on their side.'

'Yes, backed up by apathy and downright lax security,' MacFarn agreed. 'A few days before the robbery, the cleaning lady had reported finding the door to the Bedford Tower unlocked. Before that she had even found the door to the library and strongroom left open as well. On the morning of 6 July, Weirs, the Grafton Street jewellers, sent back one of the collars they had been working on. The office messenger was sent to put it with the rest of the jewels and instead found the safe unlocked and empty. The last time they had been

seen was 11 June so precisely when the theft had taken place
was unknown. The fact was that during this time Vicars had
lost his keys. They turned up at his home a few days after the
theft. The theory was that someone had "borrowed" them,
stolen the jewels, and then slid them back.'

'"Someone". It can't have been too difficult to work out
who.'

'No; at the time Vicars was sharing his home with the
young man he had appointed Dublin Herald, Francis Shackleton, an ex-officer of the South African War and brother of Sir
Ernest, the great Antarctic explorer. Shackleton had formed
a friendship with one Captain Gorges, another veteran and
hero of South Africa but also a known blackguard. Vicars was
convinced this pair were responsible and all evidence seems
to suggest that the Dublin Metropolitan Police and Scotland
Yard agreed.'

'But no arrests were made?'

'No. King Edward VII was furious at the loss. Rather than
being Republicans or Nationalists, one theory was that it was
the work of Irish monarchists hoping to restore an Irish king.
When suspicion shifted to persons closer to the Office of Arms
it was the king himself who ordered the matter closed.'

'Why, for goodness sakes?' Cress was finding this tale as
fascinating as I was.

'Because investigations revealed rumours of homosexual
rings in high government that led right to the throne itself.
The resulting scandal would have turned a loss into a disaster. Instead, Sir Arthur Vicars was dismissed his post as Chief
Herald, retired to Kilmorna, the family seat and spent the rest
of his life trying to clear his name. That wasn't very long because in 1921 the I.R.A. raided Kilmorna, fired the house and
shot Vicars on the lawn outside.'

'What about Shackleton and Gorges?'

'Gorges eventually went to jail on manslaughter charges.
Shackleton, also wanted on fraud charges, escaped abroad
to Africa. Scotland Yard eventually got extradition charges
against him, went out and brought him home.'

'Africa? Where exactly in Africa?'

MacFarn thought for a few seconds.

'Portuguese West Africa, I think. Yes, that's right. It was Angola.'

CHAPTER TWENTY-ONE

'So, KILLER O-KANE FOUND the Irish Crown jewels.' We were coasting back down the hill to the waterfront with Cress voicing my own incredulity.

'And Tracam found *him*. My guess is that he'd spent years trying to trace the jewels, finally tracked them with Shackleton to the Ataydes family in Angola only to find they'd been half-inched again at the end by Killer. The new Angolan government didn't know where they were buried so to get at the jewels Tracam had to literally buy O-Kane.' I lit a cigarette. 'Goodness knows how much they had to pay with the weapons as well.'

'A tidy sum if the trinkets are really worth what MacFarn said.' Cress looked ahead across the loch now coming back into view. 'No wonder Tracam murdered his wife for insurance. He'd need all the cash he could lay his hands on and for what? A few old stones.'

I nodded.

'That's a good point. Jewels are all very well but not worth murder and the ruination of your business empire. There has to be a deeper motive.'

'Such as?'

'Such as something MacFarn mentioned. In 1907, the British establishment were worried that this regalia of Saint Patrick might be used by a monarchist group seeking to restore an Irish king. Almost a century on, that could be the very same reason Sir John Tracam so desperately needs them now: that he and his order aren't I.R.A. at all; they're monarchists seeking to restore the Irish crown.'

Cress gave me a brief sideways glance.

'Cloud-nine land again, Mike?'

'Possibly, but think about it; the Saint Fionns go right

back to ancient Eirean and the old Irish kings. Tracam, we know, has delusions of power and megalomania. He's the honorary abbot of an ancient cult and he names his companies and ships after groups and characters in Irish mythical history. Him wanting to be King of Ireland isn't so unlikely.'

'Perhaps not,' Cress sounded a little less sceptical, 'but how could he ever achieve it? The Irish people would laugh him out of court, if you'll pardon the expression.'

I pulled to a halt by the wall alongside the quay. It was late afternoon now and the light was going.

'I'm not so sure; all over Europe there's a move back to the old monarchies. Russia is an example. Everyone is sick of all the trouble in Ireland. Perhaps the restoration of some old throne might be enough to even win over the north. If a King John could achieve a united Ireland he could well have the people with him. But you're right on one thing: it would take a pretty big act to get the world's attention.'

'You mean restoring the Irish Crown jewels to Dublin?'

I shook my head.

'That would certainly catch the people's imagination and give weight to a move back to monarchy but it wouldn't be enough to support a play for the ultimate power.' We pulled up at the water's edge. 'No, it has to be something even bigger and pretty soon too, judging by preparations.' I looked across the width of Loch Moeran towards the distant Braedon Isle. 'Sir John and his brothers have some infernal scheme hatching over in that pile of mediaeval masonry and I intend to find out what,' I leaned closer towards her, 'tonight.'

She closed her eyes.

'Oh no; you've got another plan. Mike, why don't we just go to the authorities and tell them all we now know?'

'Because they'd still not believe us and the stakes are higher now. Remember the government was offering a thousand pounds reward in 1907 but, as treasure-trove, the reward now would be in millions. A lot of financial security for both of us, Cress.'

She shook her head.

'You and your....our rewards. I hope this plan's a good one.'

'A *very* good one.' I glanced across to the old Lochmo-erantown fishing luggers. 'Can you sail a boat?'

Cress rolled her eyes.

'I have a horrible feeling I'll regret this answer but, yes, I have done some dinghy sailing.'

'Great, because tonight you're going to sail something bigger.'

'Tonight?'

'Twenty-hundred hours departure; cover-of-darkness job.' I restarted the Rover. 'I'll give you the gen as we drive.'

'To where?'

'Some secluded wood.'

'What for?'

'To hide this car and kill three hours.'

'Doing what?'

'I'm open to suggestions.'

'I bet.' She smiled impishly but as we drove out of town she stayed silent in thought. We were five mile down-loch and pulling off the road when she said, 'Talking of names, I'm not so sure Tracam is Sir John's real one. I think that when he came over here to found his business empire he decided to change his Irish family name to something more English.'

I kept the Rover going until it was out of sight of road or loch and stopped amongst the trees.

'What makes you think that?'

'Something else Pastor MacFarn said, that bit about the order being founded when Cormac MacArt was High King of Erin.'

'And....?'

'And....what's MacArt spelled backwards?'

I switched off the engine and sat in the silence. Perhaps my cloud-nine theory wasn't so fantastic after all.

THE NIGHT WAS DARK with the moon and stars lost behind a blanket of drifting stratus. A blessing to us because moonlight would have been no friend tonight and that layer of cloud would also prevent too much radiation of the day's meagre heat. This little operation was going to produce enough shivers without any help from the elements.

We were sailing just a tad west of south, straight across the gaping mouth of Loch Moeran. In spite of the cloud, the weather had stayed dry and the wind moderately west: a fair breeze that promised a fast level reach all the way there and all the way back. Lochmoerantown and the Rover were now miles astern, the latter left hidden in the trees where we'd killed a couple of passionate hours.

Like most luggers, this old wooden boat was happiest with the wind on her beam, driving on with that big tan sail sheeted well out and frothing bow and quarter waves coiling behind us. There was no cabin or cover so Cress stood beside me, huddled in her anorak.

'She's a lovely boat, Mike. I can't believe the owner let you take her without him.'

He probably wouldn't have if he'd known which he didn't. He was one of the city slickers who left his pride and joy in the hands of a local lad more than happy to make a few extra quid and no questions asked.

'Yes, and she handles a dream.' I let go the big curving tiller and eased the mainsheet slightly. 'Come on, have a go.'

'I suppose I'd better, seeing as I'm going to be single-handing in a couple of hours.' She took the helm and the instinctive glance she gave the sail's luff told me she knew what she was doing but the confidence wasn't mutual. 'You are still determined to go through with this crazy plan, I suppose?'

'Of course.' It was straightforward enough: sail up to Braedon Isle, drop me ashore and then stooge off for a couple of hours while I did my spying thing in the Monastery of Saint Fionn. Then a covert pickup and home like a bunny. A nice simple plan full of pulse-thumping possibilities that I preferred not to even consider. I pointed ahead. 'There are the lights; just keep them slightly on the port bow.'

We'd been steering a compass course so far but now, halfway across, the sparse lighting of Apprahannock was coming into view. A few pinpricks rose higher and slightly brighter than the rest: the monastery. I went for'ard to check my gear.

There wasn't much: the late driver's black habit and Mauser, a torch for signalling and a length of warp that I sincerely hoped I wouldn't need. Doing a Douglas Fairbanks up the monastery wall was definitely Plan B. The trouble was, I didn't really have a Plan A. I looked astern to Cress, windswept and competent at the tiller; this was a heavy old boat for a slim girl on her own but I'd have been more worried turning her loose in some tippy little dinghy. As long as she kept sailing with plenty of searoom she shouldn't get into much trouble. At least, that was the theory.

'Ease the sheets, Cress; slow her down a bit.'

We'd made good progress across the loch, it was still only ten and the lights were getting close. The idea had been for a silent invisible approach, not to come creaming in with the bone in her teeth. I could hear the blocks creak and the sluice at our bow dying slightly.

'Mike, there's something ahead,' she was pointing, 'just there before the island.'

I stared into the night and saw what she meant: a dark bulk in the darkness with just a solitary riding light winking its warning. In a few minutes we were abeam, sliding by just a hundred metres away and able to make out every familiar detail: the low black hull, grey superstructure with its mass of aerials and the empty helideck and faintly glimmering blue peri-lights.

'Is that what I think it is?' Cress's voice trembled slightly.

'I'm afraid so.'

MORRIGAN; what was she doing here?

WHATEVER, IT SETTLED WHICH side of Braedon Isle I wanted to land.

'Go east of the island, Cress, and bring her in on the mainland side.' That would also keep me clear of the slipway and whatever other facilities they had there. It did increase the risk of someone spotting us from Apprahannock but I'd take my chance on that against MORRIGAN's deckwatch.

'Do you think they saw us?' She nodded back to the dark outline sliding fast astern.

'I don't think so and it doesn't matter if they did; as far as they're concerned, we're just another Lochmoerantown boat out for a night's fishing.'

I spoke with a conviction I didn't feel; I could have done without this complication. MORRIGAN's presence could only mean that things were happening soon and so was my rendezvous with fate; already we were gliding past Braedon Isle with the monastery rising dark and as forbiddingly impregnable as ever.

'Ready about....lee ho!' There was a creaking of spars as Cress brought the lugger through the wind and sheeted in the mainsail. Now we were pointing straight at the island's wooded tip. 'I'll drop you there by the cover of those trees.' We crabbed in towards the shore, healed to starboard and slower through the water on this short beat to windward. I could imagine hidden eyes watching our approach and ready to pounce the second my foot touched shore.

'Perfect.' I padded sternwards long enough to give her a quick kiss. 'Be off here at 0100 and wait for the signal: two long flashes. If I'm not here within ten minutes get back to Lochmoerantown and call the cops.'

'Okay. Be careful.' The whisper in my ear came full of hot breath and promise.

I tore myself away, scampered for'ard and grabbed my gear. We touched shore as gently as that last kiss and then I was over the side in shin-deep water, throwing my kit clear and pushing off the bow. As it swung away the starboard side of the sail filled and then the lugger was gliding away with just a chuckle from her stem and a hand-blown kiss from Cress, my last sight of her in the darkness. I slid into the cover of the trees feeling suddenly very alone and wondering if any reward was really worth this.

I remained alone and glad of it; there was no welcoming committee to greet me on Braedon Isle. I was ashore, unseen, unheard and deplorably unprepared.

I SAT CROUCHED FOR a full minute, listening to make sure. Apart from the bass-drum thudding of my heart there was not a sound. Trying to remember long-lost Boy Scout lore, I loped injun-like through the wood to the opposite shore. There was a lot of undergrowth and I seemed to be kicking up enough twig-cracking noise to wake the dead. I slowed yet further in an effort not to join them.

My first objective was the slipway and, in spite of near-crawl progress, it was soon in sight through the northern fringe of the conifers. Two more paces and a thousand heart-beats brought me right to the edge of the wood.

The concrete slip used the natural slope of the isle into the loch and didn't stop short at the top but continued an-other winding three hundred yards right to the gate of the castle itself. To one side was a large area similarly concreted and bathed now in powerful arclamps. These must have been switched on since my arrival and they made it easy to see the stocky four-bladed helicopter sitting on the hard. It was the Bolkow, and beside it, dressed in an immersion suit and pac-ing impatiently was Killer O-Kane. I felt for the Mauser and gave it a reassuring squeeze.

I could see too the object of his irritation: from the castle gateway, treading with funeral slowness, came four hooded monks, one pushing a trolley, two walking beside like spec-tral pallbearers and the fourth gliding a good fifty yards astern holding what looked like a fair-sized bible. On the trolley were two cylinders.

It was easy to see all this because the arclights threw their yellow glow well up the monastery road. The road meandered a lot in its short run to the gate: it was old and Braedon Isle was liberally strewn with boulders and the original builder of ages had obviously simply wound his creation around them. One particularly large hunk of granite caused the road to make a sharp detour right by the edge of my wood. It was so pronounced that the trolley party and bible-holder would be out of sight of each other as they spanned the corner. I crept through the trees again until I was right by that turning.

The trolley party were just negotiating the bend as I got there, close enough to see that the two cylinders were nitrogen bottles for the Bolkow's emergency float inflation system. The single monk bringing up the rearguard was alongside me now with the trolley party round the bend. I stepped out, brought the broomhandle of the Mauser down on his skull and caught him in my arms before he could give so much as a groan. I glanced ahead to the trolley crew but their attention now was with Killer who was yelling oaths of impatience from the landing pad.

They didn't seem to be producing any increase in speed which was good for me because I was busy pulling off my comatose monk's waist cord and using it to rope a liberal wad of black cowl into his gaping mouth and round the tree. Then I wound my own warp around my waist, pulled on the black habit with the cowl well forward and followed the rest down the road in suitably monastic poise.

I glanced down at the book and saw that it wasn't a bible at all; it was the maintenance manual for the Bolkow 105 helicopter. The aircraft, Killer and the other three monks were only yards away now and obviously waiting for me and my manual. If they spoke to me I was sunk but curiosity and lack of any escape route anyway kept me going.

Killer spoke first.

'Okay, we've wasted enough time already; let's get those bottles changed over.' Two monks lifted the cylinders off the trolley. Nitrogen bottles did need recharging periodically but this was an odd time and place to do it. His next words explained all. 'Go easy with those things; one whiff and we'll all be goddam bye-byes for good.' Those bottles weren't containing nitrogen but some form of nerve gas.

Killer produced tools and disconnected the stainless-steel

lines on the aircraft bottles. One of the monks gestured towards the manual but Killer waived me away.

'I don't need no goddam book; just give me a hand to get these things off.' While the bottles were changed I kept a relieved distance and my cowled face in the shadows. I'd already worked out how the gas would be dispersed: instead of reconnecting the float system to the bottles, Killer had simply jubilee-clipped the open pipes to the skids. Now, with the float-system armed, just a squeeze of the switch on the collective would have whatever nasties those bottles contained, flowing fast and free at 2800 p.s.i. straight into the atmosphere. It was an ingenious, simple and very deadly mod.

The job was just completed when, from the monastery, there came the mournful tolling of a bell. One of the monks flicked a surprisingly complex timepiece from his sleeve.

'Midnight compline, brothers. Time to go.' They formed single file and I joined them, hands clasped before us, winding our ghostly way back up the monastery road. As we passed the corner I listened. A low moan was coming through the trees but it wasn't my monk; it was a rising wind that had me thinking of Cress helming alone out there on the loch.

Right now, I wished so much I were with her; ahead the dark towering geometry of Saint Fionns rose in castle-like splendour, its massive oak doors drawing closer by the second. A small wicket gate opened and we bowed through. As I brought up the rear, cowl well forward and my heart booming louder than the bell, it slammed shut behind me with an ominous finality. For better or worse, I was in Saint Fionns' monastery.

I had a bad feeling it was for worse.

CHAPTER TWENTY-TWO

WE FILED ACROSS A quadrangle formed by buildings that were an inward extension of the castle walls. Lights glowed dimly behind vaulted tracery casements while from the high tower the bell continued its steady call to compline.

I assumed we were heading for the chapel and wondering how I was going to cope with complex Latin responses and, even worse, whether I'd have to drop my cowl. I prepared to peel off but instead we entered a broad-fronted building as granite-old as the rest and incongruously echoing to the thud and stamp of moving bodies.

It was a gymnasium full from stone floor to vaulted ceiling with the latest fitness technology. We floated through while men in black tracksuits and bulging torsos completed a session of unarmed combat. If there were any Friar Tucks in Saint Fionns, they weren't here.

Nor in the next room either where the smell was of sweat and gunoil and bright lights glinted off blued-metal Skorpions and the bare skin tonsures of monks talking in incomprehensible Gaelic. Again we passed on through into a room containing, for me, something even deadlier.

Changing lockers. Monks were donning habits but my group was stripping theirs, presumably for a quick shower before compline. This was no place for hairy-headed Tempest but if I hesitated they'd notice me for sure. Instead I kept on going, through a far door and back into the darkened quad. I slid into some dark shadows to slow my pulse and settle my thoughts.

Minutes later the whole gang of about fifty came padding past in perfect double file, silent and ghostlike and enroute to chapel. I shrunk back into the stonework, my nerves at full stretch and more so later when spiritual cadences came drifting back to soak the ancient castle walls with an eerie unreality. The brothers of Saint Fionns were as solidly devout as their fighting forbears and undeniably better equipped. We were up against formidable forces, that was for sure: trained commandos were one thing but give them religious zeal as well and they'd be virtually unstoppable.

But what were they training for? With the whole order now seemingly wrapped in their midnight prayer session, it seemed the time to find out. I didn't know how long compline lasted but the sooner I got started, the better. I took stock of my surroundings.

At the seaward end of the quadrangle the tiered battle-ments climbed skywards, crowned by the impressive array of aerials which we'd seen from the shore. If there was anything to discover in this depressing pile of masonry it would be in those upper rooms where lights burned dimly behind heavy curtains. Staying in the shadows, I moved around the quad, grateful that the brothers of long ago had chosen black as the colour of their order.

The main door, when I reached it, was of solid oak and as formidable as the mediaeval day it was made. I tried the handle and it opened. Not so illogical really: with Braedon Castle impregnable in its own right, the order could afford to relax internal security....until tonight. I went on in.

The first level was bare stone flooring leading to various uninteresting rooms. They included a well-stocked dispensary and one austere office bearing the door title CELLARER. I made my stealthy way up the dark oak staircase to the next level.

At first glance it seemed as uninteresting as the ground though I was obviously ascending the corridors of power. The plates on the doors of the first two rooms said PRIOR and SUB-PRIOR. I glanced inside each and found them un-rewarding and empty. The same couldn't be said of the third and last room. From the other side of the closed door came the squeals and background static of radios; this was Saint Fionn's communications centre. With my ear to the door I could hear the changing voice traffic as an operator swept the frequency bands. Obviously even midnight prayers didn't stop the brothers maintaining radio watch. In there would be answers. I felt for the Mauser; should I just walk in and get them? Better to recce the top floor first before setting off some hue and cry. I retreated back along the corridor and on up the stairs.

At the top, all monastic austerity ended. Here bare floors gave way to rich pile carpets. I padded silently along through half open doors, my passage lit by ornate chandeliers and brass picture lights above heavy works in oil that lined the walls. Whoever occupied this penthouse hadn't kicked off too many of life's little comforts. Obviously the domain of Sir John Tracam. Where was Saint Fionns' honorary abbot? Presumably at chapel with the rest. I moved on into what was obviously his lounge.

It was snug and warm with a log fire roaring in a big stone fireplace. Beyond the country sofas and antique sidetables sat a fine Georgian desk, its surface littered with books and papers. Beneath this clutter lay an Admiralty chart.

It was of this area; I found Loch Moeran and Braedon Isle and a trackline drawn northwest, fifteen miles out into the centre of the North Minch. Here, in the stretch of relatively sheltered water between mainland Scotland and the Western Isles, the trackline had been ringed in red with six figures pencilled alongside: 250835. A position? Couldn't be. A military time and date group perhaps? That made more sense. If so it meant that something was going to happen here at 8:35 a.m. on the 25th of this month: tomorrow. I flicked through other papers: tidetables, reduction tables, weather forecasts, general nautical data but nothing to indicate what was going to happen in less than nine hours. My eyes dropped down alongside the desk to where an ancient steel safe sat solid and inviting. I tried the handle; it might have been ancient but it was just as impossibly locked. Before I could try the desk drawer for a key I heard voices coming up the stairs. One was a woman's, high raised and angry. I looked around desperately for another door and saw only ancient wood panelling.

THEN I SAW A brass handle; a door was built into the panelling and nigh on invisible. There was also a brass plate: GARD-EROBE. I hoped no-one was guarding the robes right now, turned the handle and went on in.

Strange names in these monasteries; the garderobe was just a toilet but that gave it two redeeming features: a door that locked and a small window opening out into the castle wall. I pulled the door behind me to within a crack of fully closed and watched as they came in.

He was ensconced in black habit and I'd only seen his photo in the papers but I recognised immediately that fine aquiline profile framed in thick white beard and hair: Sir John Tracam. I'd only seen her in the flesh once before on a rain-soaked apron but she still carried that brassy air of flaunted sexiness: Madam Lena LeVoy, the absent seer of Hackney Marshes. Her husky east London accent came as no surprise.

'I tell you, I'm sick of this.' She flung herself onto a sofa with one half of her leopard-skin leggings dangling over the arms. 'I didn't give up a good business down south just to come and freeze in this old morgue. How long do I have to put up with this?'

'All in good time, my dear; all in good time.' Sir John's urbane manner was in sharp contrast to that of his mistress but it cut no ice for all that.

'Don't you "my dear" me.' She stood up defiantly with hands on shapely hips. 'You promised me glitter and riches and all I've seen so far is bald monks and stone walls.'

'Then perhaps these will give you something on which to contemplate.' Sir John took a ring of keys from his waist cord, unlocked the safe and withdrew two wooden boxes. Opening the lids, he placed them on the table in front of Lena.

'Strewth!' Her long fingers dipped into both boxes and even in the subdued lighting, flashes of brilliance sparked from the small clusters she held in each hand. 'They're beautiful. Are those real diamonds, Johnny?'

Tracam nodded.

'Indeed they are, my dear. The eight points of the star

are all in Brazilian and that shamrock in the centre is set on a ruby cross. The badge is made from diamonds, emeralds and rubies also.

Lena held the jewels up to her yellow sweatshirt.

'Cor, Johnny, these are trinkets fit for a....a....'

'....Queen.' Tracam slid the jewels from Lena's reluctant grasp and placed them reverently back into their boxes. 'And so they shall be, my dear; so they shall be.'

'Yeh, but when?' Lena wasn't so easily appeased. 'I'm not staying here forever and die of boredom.'

There was obviously a limit to even Tracam's patience. He banged his fist hard down on the desk.

'You will leave here when I say you can and not before.'

'Oh, yer; and how you going to stop me then? Deal with me like you did your old woman?'

'What do you mean by that?' Tracam's voice had hardened to whetted titanium.

'You know what I mean. All that kidnap business was so much bunkum. It was you who had her done in; you an that Charlie Smallbright.'

'You have no proof of that.'

'Oh no? Well, we'll see. In the meantime, you play monks if you want to but I'm off south for a bit of fun and sun. Call me when ye'r ready to give me the good life in exchange for my closed trap.' She swung on her heels and almost cannoned into a figure who had silently come in behind her.

'Hi, Lena. Going someplace?' He advanced into the room and I noticed Lena back away nervously. Here was one man she feared and with good reason.

'O-Kane; what you doin' here?'

'Just seeing if I can help which is more than you seem to be doing.'

'Yer,' I admired Lena's quick recovery, 'well if you want to help you can make sure that frantic palmtree of yours is ready to fly me out just as soon as I'm packed,' She strode out slamming the door behind her with a force that shook even Braedon's rugged walls.

'That woman could be big trouble.' Killer slumped in a chair opposite Tracam's desk. His eyes fell on the jewels. 'Heh, you've been playing with the stones.' He picked up the Star but the Fionn's honoury abbot went to grab it back.

'When I want your advice, O-Kane, I'll ask for it. You were hired to fly my helicopter, train my men and fly the operation, not to be my domestic advisor.'

Killer pulled his hand and the Star away.

'Who you kidding, Tracam? You bought me out of that stinking jail to get your hands on these and for that reason only. My other skills were just so much bonus thrown into the bargain.'

'Yes, well you haven't covered yourself with glory yet, have you? Remember it was you who let Tempest and the girl slip through our fingers.'

'Tempest!' Just the mention of my name seemed to push Killer's ire up ten points. 'I'll get that mother.' He tossed the Star back onto the desk. 'Any sign of that missing station wagon of yours yet?'

'No,' Tracam sat back subdued, Killer's point hitting home, 'and you're probably right about Lena. It was a mistake bringing her up here. I behaved like a fool.'

Killer allowed a patronising smile; he'd won again and he knew it.

'Everyone needs a little fling occasionally, Tracam, and she did serve one purpose: if your old woman hadn't found out about your little affair and threatened to blow the whistle on this lot you'd have never had her snuffed and got that insurance.'

'That was your idea, O-Kane, and don't you forget it.' There was a hint of remorse in the old boy's voice.

'Right, but that six million sure came in handy at the end, didn't it?'

Tracam shook his head.

'It did indeed; the Angolan government virtually cleaned me out. There was the price of your release and yet more bribes to get you and the jewels out of the country not to mention the cost of all those small arms and mines. The insurance settlement allowed me to at least pay off some of my most pressing creditors but, just the same, the Tracam Group is virtually insolvent.'

'But for a good cause.' Killer leaned across. 'After tomorrow, you can dictate your own terms.'

'If all goes well.'

'It will.'

Tracam picked up the Star and Badge and turned them in his fingers.

'To the Irish people these will symbolise a return to the ancient order. After tomorrow a new star will shine over that blessed isle and once again a united Ireland will have peace.'

'And we shall have money.' Killer was looking at the old man through cynical narrowed eyes. 'When you've got your kingdom, Tracam, don't forget who got you there.'

Tracam put the insignia back on his desk. He must have realised that greed always formed a part of Killer's motivation but his tone was level again for all that.

'You'll be well rewarded, O-Kane, never fear. Just make sure you don't fail tomorrow. Is everything ready?'

'One hundred percent.' Killer gave a mock salute.

'Good; and we still have some mines on board?'

'Two, as ordered.' He nodded towards the sheaf of radio signals on the abbot's desk. 'Do you think we'll need them?'

'Only if they pursue us too closely.' Tracam flicked through them. 'Communications indicate everything is running as predicted. She should be in position right on schedule.' He brushed the papers aside. 'Return to MORRIGAN and await my activation signal.'

'Roger.' Killer jumped up in best fighting manner, headed for the door but then paused and turned. 'How about that fortune-telling bitch? Want me to deal with her?'

Tracam paused for just three seconds.

'Yes.'

That was good enough for Killer and he was gone.

I glanced at my watch: thirty minutes after midnight; time

for me to be gone too if I was to keep my date with Cress. But how? The future King of Ireland seemed content to gloat over his jewels. Easy enough to neutralise him but how to keep it quiet and, even if I did, how to get past the main gate? One lone monk going out was bound to attract some attention. My short term options seemed reduced to one: the loo window.

I eased the door closed completely and locked it behind me, stripped off the habit and unwound the warp. The window opened just enough but down the sheer west wall of Braedon Castle to the rocky foreshore below was a good thirty feet. I was gambling that Tracam's hearing would be past its prime but just the same I worked like a ghost in a library, hitching my warp to the toilet and feeding the rest through the window. I looked down and saw the warp was short by a third.

Ten feet was a long drop onto solid rock but the time for options was long past. I jammed the Mauser tighter into my belt, heaved myself through the opening and started down, hoping the castle plumbing was as solid as the rest of the building. If it wasn't I'd be plunging down its venerable walls with a hundredweight of kaze behind me.

It wasn't a descent that would have won me any commando badge. In the gusting wind, I revolved like a vertigoed puppet, bumping and scraping down the rough-hewn granite with the only consolation being that it wouldn't be for long.

It wouldn't have been either if the monk hadn't come around the corner.

HE WAS BLACK-COWLED AND ghostlike except few ghosts carried Skorpion SMGs slung over their shoulders. I should have realised they maintained a watch on the shore and this was a bad way to find out. I stopped my slither at the warp end, ten feet above him and my muscles fit to bust.

He stopped too, right there beneath me, sat himself down on a rock and gazed seaward. How long he intended staying, I didn't know but probably longer than my arms could hold. While they were still in their sockets and I had something to cushion my fall I let go and as I did so he looked up.

All that karate had given him good reflexes and he was almost on his feet when I hit him with both of mine. He gave a bone-cracking gasp of agony and went down again with the Skorpion flying. This only made us equal because his shoulders had given me a good jarring and sent my weapon the same way as his. We ended up face to face, his a mask of contorted agony from whatever had gone snap when I hit him.

He wasn't fit to fight but he seemed all set to holler which was just as deadly. I removed the option with the first thing to hand: a good chunk of Braedon Isle rock straight to the forehead. He sank back without so much as a whimper and I paused long enough only to recover his Skorpion and two spare mags. He wouldn't be needing them again if his stillness was anything to go by but he'd shortened my time to rendezvous with Cress to a mere ten minutes. I set off around the castle, my feet still hurting from one contact and my hopes set on avoiding another.

To that end I kept to the landward side, avoided the lights of the slip and was soon in the cover of the trees. It should have been a comfort except they were bending now as the wind howled through them. Horrible doubts were only strengthened when I reached the loch and found it boatless. Where was Cress?

I squinted desperately into the night across spume-flecked waters and saw a shape just darker than the darkness, materialising into a boat, spray sheeting from its hull and that big tan lugsail drawing ever closer. I pulled the torch from my pocket and heard the monastery bell start to ring.

Not the slow tolling of compline this time but a fast urgent call to arms. I aimed the torch towards the lugger and flashed. Nothing; the thing must have bust in the fall. No time either to try and fix it because unseen bodies were already crashing towards me through the trees. I dropped the torch and reached for the Skorpion but even as I did so a hooded figure burst through the undergrowth right on top of me.

CHAPTER TWENTY-THREE

IF IT WAS A shock to me it was an even greater one for the monk. He gave a shriek that was almost girl-like unless....I grabbed his cowl and pulled it back.

'Lena LeVoy.' She went to vent another scream but this time I got my hand over her mouth in time. 'Shut up.'

Hazel eyes stared into mine, quickly mellowing from stark fear to limited trust. I eased my hand away and she took a deep breath and glanced back over her shoulder.

'Those monks....the men from this monastery....they're trying to kill me.' There was a bulge under her habit and panic in the cockney.

'I know and I'll do it myself if you don't keep your voice down. Hand me that torch.' It wasn't difficult to find because the second bash had brought it to life, its beam shining into the undergrowth. Cupping my hands over the lens, I aimed a couple of long flashes at the lugger and hoped like hell Cress would see them.

Even if she did, would she get here in time? Above the tolling bell and wind in the trees, men were shouting. It was Lena they were looking for but that would make little difference in the end. I glanced again at the lugger, saw thankfully that she was slapping towards us but wished her nearer just the same.

'Who are you?' Lena's whispered voice was a mixture of relief and suspicion.

'A friend....almost.' Cress was close now, luffing off the speed for the final creep in. I grabbed Lena by the scruff of her habit and pulled her with me into the frothing waters, arctic cold but worth the discomfort if it prevented Cress running hard aground. We waded deeper, me pulling Lena with one hand and holding the Skorpion clear with the other, she still gripping whatever she had hidden beneath the habit. Soon we were breast-deep and shivering and me wondering if Cress would miss our small targets in the darkness and run us down?

I shouldn't have worried; seconds later the lugger brought up right beside us, sail and blocks rattling like the chains of Hades while ominous lights appeared on the near shore.

'In!' I heaved Lena, heavy in sodden habit, over the gunwale, slung the Skorpion in after her, kicked off the bow and tumbled aboard. 'Bear away, Cress, for Pete's sake.' To add encouragement, a burst of automatic fire came from shoreward.

Splinters of wood flew from somewhere amidships accompanied by a muffled scream from the bundle of sodden habit that was already diving into the bilges. I grabbed the Skorpion and fired a wild burst in return, at the same time stumbling aft to check on Cress.

'Mike; are you okay?' She was pumping the tiller for all she was worth, working the boat onto a starboard tack that would fill the sail and get us moving.

I added my weight to hers.

'Just fine so long as we put some space between here and there.' By now a powerful flashlight was fixing us in its beam. We instinctively ducked as another burst of hot 7.62 came flying along it producing a line of jagged holes in the mainsail that at least was now filling. The rattling of demented blocks subsided into disciplined silence, the boat heeled slightly and we pulled away.

'Keep her jibing round, Cress....straight downwind.' A broad reach would have had us going faster but that would have put us beam on and taken us close to Apprahannock. I wanted open water and the smallest target possible. Another ripple of flashes appeared on the shore accompanied by a buzz of staccato fire, a line of small splashes ending at our waterline and the ominous crack of splintering woodwork. Once again there was a muffled scream from the bottom of the boat.

'Who's that?' Cress had the tiller hard over.

'You'll find out; just keep this boat turning.' There was

more rattle of running rigging as we put our stern through the wind. 'Jibe-oh, watch for the blocks.' A second later the big loose-footed sail came winging over and the boat rolled onto her new port tack. More important, Braedon Isle and its angry order were slipping fast astern. There was a final desultory burst of fire, hissing splashes appeared in our already creaming wake and we were away.

'Are we safe?' A peroxide blonde head was finally emerging from the bilges.

'It's her,' Cress nodded towards the woman rolling something into the black habit she had just pulled off to reveal see-through blouse and cream skin-tight leggings, 'the fortune-teller from the fair; Madame Something-or-other. What's she doing here?'

'LeVoy and I'll tell you later. For the moment let's bring this old tub onto a broad reach and course for Lochmoerantown.' With hell itself on our tail and a force-eight crossing of the loch in the offing, the last thing I needed were females catting each other. We were off the wind now, our quarter waves curling away on either side as we crashed through the chop on the lugger's fastest point of sailing.

The faster the better as far as I was concerned: there were many miles to go and the lads back there had some pretty fancy equipment, not least, the two fast RIBS from *MORRIGAN*. It wouldn't take them long to narrow our slender gap. We were past the ship now but it hadn't done my confidence much good to see her radar aerials turning their all-seeing sweeps. Neither did Lena's next words.

'We're taking in water.'

We were too, at the waterline from that last burst to hit us.

'Well don't just sit there crying about it. Stuff that habit over the holes.'

Lena seemed loathe to unroll her precious habit but she turned her back to us, slid something into her blouse and the black cloak into the leaking planks.

'Will that stop it?'

'No, but it'll slow the flow.'

But for how long? I kept that doubt to myself and concentrated on steering for a heavy rain squall that lay across our track. Normally that was the last thing I would have done but tonight I blessed the fast-deteriorating weather whose evil gusts constantly threatened to put us on our beam ends. But heavy rain meant bad radar definition and that black storm ahead would probably defeat even MORRIGAN's sophisticated gear. We plunged on with the wind screaming in the rigging. This was my night for screams and presently I heard another: the fast approach of high-revving outboards.

CRESS HAD HEARD IT too and together we looked back towards Braedon Isle. Speeding out from the slip was an all-black dory, bow high, already on the step and sure to be alongside in minutes. Could we lose them in the rain squall? I looked ahead at the precipitation still half a mile off and realised we hadn't a hope.

'They're goin' to nab us for sure.'

I was hoping Lena's stars had got it wrong but I had limited earthly assets to prove it: the Skorpion and two spare mags plus anything else in the lugger's lockers. I went rummaging, found a Very signal pistol and half-a-dozen cartridges, went to get back on my feet, thought better of it and crawled back to the stern.

'Cress, for all the enemy know, it's just you and Lena in here; she was the one they were chasing.' I glanced at our passenger who obviously thought I was going to throw her to the wolves and then at Cress who obviously thought it would be a good idea if we did. They were both wrong. 'I'm going to keep lying down here and I want you, Cress, to start sailing badly and let them come alongside. Play the helpless female,' I glanced back at Lena, 'both of you.'

'Mike....' Cress had guessed my plan and didn't like it.

'Our only chance, Cress. Start handling this thing as though the weather's getting the better of you.'

She bit her lip and nodded and straight away started working the mainsheets so that one second we were heeled hard over with the gunwale slopping green and the next rolling upright with the tan sail luffing its guts out. The result was a drastic slowing of our speed and the ever faster approach of the dory.

I couldn't see it but I could hear the engines down-revving and knew they were almost alongside. A silent nod from Cress confirmed it.

'Okay, heave-to, put your hands up and start pleading.'

She pushed the helm over, let go the mainsheet until the sail was flapping like linen on washday and gave her most pitiful female best.

'Don't shoot. Please don't shoot.'

'We give up. Don't hurt us for Gord's sake.' I wasn't sure whether Lena was acting or not.

Slowly and silently I cocked the Skorpion and slid the selector to automatic.

'How many, Cress?'

She kept her hands high but raised two fingers slightly. Good odds unless they came in firing. I held my breath until there was the bump of their hull against ours.

'Down; both of you.'

I leapt to my feet as the girls dropped and came face-to-face with two black-shrouded figures holding Skorpions just like mine except theirs were silent whereas mine was already spitting a stream of hot 7.62 lead. The black habits stained bright red and dropped like a pair of unstitched rag dolls.

'Get us under-weigh....quick.' I was yelling like Captain Bligh but I needed to shake them both from the shock of another bloody carnage. They pulled themselves to their feet with looks that said I wouldn't be getting a Nobel Peace Prize for a long time yet. That didn't matter. What did was that Cress was already hauling in the dripping mainsheet and filling the sail.

The dory, with its still-idling engines, drifted slowly astern. On the wind came the unmistakable smell of petrol; obviously some of my rounds had found their tank. I loaded the Very, took deliberate aim and sent a comet-like ball of pulsating phosphorous right into it. There was an eruption of flame and a blast of heat that had us ducking twenty yards away. In the centre of this conflagration, two lifeless forms curled and shrivelled while the cartridge still spilled out its blood-red heart. No Viking could ask for better.

There was just a wisp of steam to mark its end as we slipped into the squall.

'So, WHAT'S THIS BIG show they're planning tomorrow?'

We were clearing the northern edge of the storm, battered, soaking wet but free from further intercepts. Between the vicious gusts, we'd managed to maintain the semblance of a compass heading, kept the inflow of water to bailable proportions and watched the blessed lights of Lochmoerantown come into sight. Time enough to give Madame LeVoy the third degree.

She paused from pouring another bailerful over the side.

'I haven't the faintest idea, darlin'.' Lena was far from glamorous in the dawn light, her blonde thatch like a charwoman's mop and an expression that said sailing and questions at five in the morning were regarded with the same equal loathing. 'You don't think he told me anythin' do you?'

'Well you slept with Tracam didn't you?' Cress's tone didn't add to the morning's warmth.

'Yeh, and that's about all we did.' Lena scooped another load of Loch Moeran from the bilges.

I almost felt sorry for her.

'How did you get mixed up with this crowd anyway?'

She shrugged.

'I was doin' me fortune telling thing at a funfair near London. It was owned by a little creep called Smallbright. He was into dope I'm sure because....'

'We know all about Smallbright,' I interrupted shortly. 'How did you meet Tracam?'

Lena shook her head.

'One night Charlie invites me over to his van cos he's got

some gent who wants his palm read for a bit of a giggle. Turns
out to be Johnny....Sir John Tracam. Never seen him before
but apparently Charlie had some dock or something up north
that Johnny wanted to use...'

'Langsden Priory; we know all about that too.' I interrupted. 'So, it was Smallbright that introduced you?'

She nodded.

'Yeh, and right impressed I was; not Charlie's sort at all.
They obviously had some bent gig goin' together but Johnny
was a gentleman for all that and I could see he fancied me
rotten. When I'd done my thing he took my palm, pretended
to read it and said he could see wealth coming my way. About
time too, I thought and that's how we got started.'

No thanks to any Cupid. I could imagine Charlie Smallbright steering old Tracam into this illicit romance solely as a
way of creaming more cash. Obviously Cress wasn't impressed
either. She took the bailer from Lena and sloshed some water,
not a little going over our passenger.

'Sorry....you knew, of course, that he was already married?'

If it was meant to rattle Lena, it failed.

'Course I did, love. Right naggy bitch she was too by all
accounts. Naturally, she found out about our little fling after
a few months and shortly after that she was kidnapped and
murdered.'

'And you weren't suspicious?'

Lena rolled lovely hazel eyes.

'Not half I wasn't but I was sure from the start that it was
Smallbright that had snuffed her. While all this is goin' on,
Johnny tells me it would be better if I cleared off to his castle
in Scotland. Sounded all right to me 'cept it turns out to be a
bleedin' monkery.'

'But you never discovered their grand plan?'

The fortune teller shrugged again.

'Didn't even try. Johnny sometimes talked about some
crazy idea to become a king and me his queen but I just put

that down to fantasy. He did have this weird thing about power, you know.'

'We do. So you got bored and did a runner?'

She nodded vigorously.

'Too right I did. I'm not a complete sprucer, you know, when it comes to the occults. The vibes were all wrong and spirits were tellin' me that if I didn't get out soon it would be never at all.'

'Another ten minutes, and you could have told them they were right.' I eased the mainsheet and bore away slightly down-loch. 'Killer O-Kane was all set to send you the way of Lady Tracam.'

'That creep.' Lena shuddered. 'I felt as much so I grabbed this hooded thing for disguise and beat it. I guess he found me gone and raised the alarm.' She smiled sweetly and touched my hand. 'That's when I ran into you, darlin'.'

'Michael, I thought we were going to Lochmoerantown?' I'd altered course and so had the conversation.

'I've changed my mind. We'll take her down-loch and beach her close to where we hid the Rover. It'll save time. Whatever it is Tracam's planning is going to happen at 0835 fifteen miles northwest of here in The Minch. Something big and nasty too; they've got stun-gas on the helicopter.'

'Stun-gas?' In the cold light, Cress's hair was spray-streaked across a face pinched white by cold but she still looked as lovely as Lena did sexy.

'Yeh, and those two mines are still on MORRIGAN.'

'Good grief; for what?'

'I've no idea, but Tracam said one curious thing to Killer: he confirmed that there were " some still onboard".'

'So?'

'So, that indicates there might have been others. You said yourself there seemed space for more. If so, where were they laid?'

Cress shrugged.

'Perhaps in the southern North Sea before we escaped.'

'Possible, but nothing on the news and I can't see the

point now anyway. What this lot are planning is a whole lot more than just disruption. Of course, they may have dropped them in the Western Isles on the way down but that seems just as unlikely. The gas on that helio indicates they want to capture rather than destroy.'

'Capture what?'

I shook my head again.

'I don't know, Cress?'

Cress ran a hand through her hair and wiped some spray from her face.

'The nuclear submarines south of here at Faslane; do you think they're going to try and highjack one? All this participation in demonstrations might have just been a cover for recceing the base and its security. Trident Ploughshares got in so why shouldn't they?'

I shook my head.

'Impossible. From what you told me, those activists swam into the base. A couple of individuals might just get away with that but Tracam is planning something on a far greater scale. With his hardware, he'd be sussed and the security system on high alert before he got within miles of the base. There are patrol boats and Marine commandos on constant guard. He wouldn't stand a chance.And, anyway, the Brothers maintain a listening watch on marine frequencies which indicates they're after something already at sea.'

'Could he capture a nuclear sub out in the Irish Sea, well clear of the base?'

'Not a chance; those nuclear boats stay submerged all the time. Even a megalomaniac like Tracam wouldn't try anything as wacky as that.'

I knew I was talking sense but, even so, there had been something in what Cress had said that had struck a nerve. The trouble was, I couldn't think what and I didn't have time to give it further thought because we were abeam the woods concealing the Rover and it was time to get landing. I put the helm over and handed it to Cress who eased us in while I jumped ashore with the headrope. Lena grabbed her sodden habit from the bilges and scrambled ashore with Cress close behind.

'What do you want to bring that horrible thing for?'

'Souvenir, darlin'.'

Why not? I warped the old lugger to a tree and five minutes had the Rover located and us piling aboard. With the heat full up we were soon blasting down the lonely road to Fort William.

'So, what's the plan, skipper?' Cress was combing tangled hair while Lena sat silent but apparently warmer in the back.

I pulled a cigarette from the pack on the dashboard and lit up.

'The police at Fort William, I guess, and hope they'll believe us.'

'Why should they; we're still not sure ourselves what Tracam is up to. Telling them we want to report the King of Ireland isn't guaranteed to enforce our credibility.' She threw the comb back on the dashboard. 'If we could only give them some idea of what plan he's hatching it would help. Why participate in peaceful protests inland when you're planning a military action in The Minch. It just doesn't make sense.'

It still didn't make sense to me either so we sped on in silence along narrow roads slick with rain, wooded Highland grandeur rising impressively to port and the rapidly narrowing waters of Loch Moeran to starboard. I reached for another cigarette

'You should throw those things away.'

For a second I thought she was talking about the cigarettes and then realised she meant the Skorpion and Very pistol down by my feet.

'Not yet; we may still need them.' I lit the second cigarette from the first, a sure sign I was worrying.

For one thing, the time was 0725: a mere hour and ten minutes to zero. For another there was the sound. It was getting closer. It was the rhythmic thump and scream of an approaching helicopter.

CHAPTER TWENTY-FOUR

'STREWTH, ITS THAT BLEEDIN' O-Kane comin' after us.'

But Lena's stars were very wrong again; I wasn't into mystic forces but I did know my helicopters and this one had a screaming gearbox made by Aerospatialle. Seconds later we saw the machine and I was right. It was a Llama, an open-frame helicopter that compensated for austere lines by sheer power and strength.

Cress peered up as the machine went banking overhead.

'What on earth is he doing?'

From the helicopter's external load hook hung a five-foot cable and, on the end of that, a hopper. As we watched, the pilot lined up on the hillside forestry and spewed a snowfall of white crystals on the trees fifty feet below.

'Strewth, he's crop-spraying.'

Lena was half-right.

'Top-dressing actually: spreading granular phosphate on the plantations to help growth.' In fact, this was about the only work left for the old crop-dusting outfits in our new green times but I was wondering if this particular machine might do the country an even greater service yet. I peered ahead. 'Let's find out where he's landing.'

'You're not thinking of stealing it by any chance?' Miss Dysart was starting to know me too well.

'Not steal, Cress, borrow. It's the only way we'll get to Fort William in time and we'll certainly get more attention when we do.'

They didn't argue and I kept the Rover gunning inland. The loading pad wouldn't be far away because the whole advantage of helicopters was to keep positioning to the minimum. In another minute the stream of white granules from this one abruptly stopped and then the pilot was winging her round and beelining back for another hook-up. A mile ahead, he descended and disappeared behind some trees. I followed.

By the time we drew level, the Llama was already lifting with another load. I pulled the Rover off the road and got out.

'You girls stay here while I do a recce.' Still no argument. I was soon back.

'As I thought, only three ground crew in a clear area behind those trees.' I pulled open the rear door. 'Lena, can you drive this thing?' She gave a quick nervous nod. 'Good, because I want you to take it a few hundred yards down the road and run it off. Nothing too dramatic, just make it look like you've skidded off and need a push. Then I want you to make for that pad and wait for the helicopter to land and stop his rotor. He'll do that eventually for a break. When that happens, come into the open and plead for help. Get as many of them as possible to come and give you a push. Can you do that?'

She gave another nod.

'How about you?'

'That's when I'll do my bit and grab the helicopter. Right then,' I pulled out the Skorpion and Very pistol and held the door open for Lena, 'in you get. Cress, you come with me.'

'I was beginning to wonder if there was a part for me in this little drama.'

Women can be so damn touchy but I ignored it.

'They'll probably leave someone with the helicopter so I'll need you to cover while I get the thing wound up.' I'd actually been thinking of leaving them both with the Rover but that would have been a combination more lethal than Killer's mines.

'You mean point that thing at someone.' She was looking at the Skorpion like it was something the cat had dragged in.

'Yeh, but pointing is all you'll be doing. Keep the selector on *safe* and don't touch a thing.' I lit a final cigarette and jammed the Very in my belt. 'Okay, girls, let's go.' We watched Lena drive off and then headed for the wood.

It took us a little while to reach the pad because we took a circular route that brought us in from the rear; opposite to where Lena would eventually make her dramatics.

'How long is it going to take us to fly to Fort William?' With Lena gone, Cress's manner was back to its old warmness.

'About thirty-five minutes.' I glanced at my watch: 0750. Even in the Llama it was going to be a close-run thing. I turned and took Cress's hand. 'You okay?'

She smiled just a trifle sheepishly and nodded.

'I think so.'

We were on the far side of the operating area now with everything as I'd seen it twenty-five minutes before: three men loading a hopper for the next hook-up, sacks of fertilizer, drums of fuel. It wouldn't be long before he was needing more of the latter: fuel was always kept low on this kind of work.

In fact he needed it sooner than I would have liked. On his next arrival the pilot waived away the hook-up crew and brought the Llama in to a full landing. Straight after touchdown the big Artouste engine came to ground idle and the three-blade rotor to a standstill. I kept my fingers crossed that Lena would make it. Already the ground crew were running out the fuel hose.

Unfortunately they never pumped so much as a gallon before our girl made her appearance. I cursed myself for not telling her to let them refuel first. Too late now; her hysterics were getting the attention of the crew but it was the torn blouse and Page Three exposure beneath that brought work to a halt. The Llama's engine died to sudden silence as the pilot shut down for his own piece of Lena's up-front action.

'What a tart.' Cress's whisper didn't hide her feelings.

'Yeh, but she's getting results.' Too much result, in fact: by now the whole crew, pilot included, were piling into their van with the damsel in distress and departing the site.

I watched them go with mixed feelings: the helicopter was ours but it was shutdown and devoid of fuel. Left running with some crew, the rescue team wouldn't have thought too much of it lifting off. Now, as that 870 horsepower burst to screaming life, it would have the whole lot wheeling back in five minutes flat and before that we'd have to dish ourselves some gas. I went to the pump and hose.

'Oh no.'

'What?' Cress was beside me.

'The nozzle is locked.' I should have expected it: everything on these remote locations was kept chained down and this was probably the first refuel of the day. The key to this setup was probably a mile down the road by now. I went over to the Llama and flicked the battery switch. The gauges sprang to life including fuel which was near enough on the redline. 'Almost out.'

'Can't we saw through the lock or something?'

'Not before that crew return.' I was thinking of something that we'd passed a few miles back down the road. 'Get in, Cress.'

'We're taking off with virtually no fuel. Where?'

'You'll see. Strap in.'

She did while I shoved the Skorpion and Very down by her feet, flicked the generator and starter and watched the engine gauges come to ear-splitting life. The Artouste had a fully automatic sequence and thirty seconds had it self-sustaining. I eased open the throttle and let the clutch get the rotor turning as well, at the same time wondering what effect it was having down by the Rover. I hoped I'd never find out. With the rotor at its full 330 r.p.m. I pulled the pitch and as I did so the van came screaming back into the clearing.

The sight of their livelihood getting light on its skids certainly gave that dusting crew an extra turn of speed. They came sprinting towards me at a rate that made me forget that French helicopter rotors turned the other way. As I jerked into the hover I put in wrong pedal causing the Llama to yaw around the clearing like a demented gyro, its buzzing tail rotor effectively scattering her late crew.

Late in more ways than one; we were climbing away now, vertically spinning out of the clearing while I jammed in opposite pedal trying to stop the yaw. Clear of the treetops, I pushed the twitching helicopter into forward flight and things started to stabilize. At eighty knots, we headed for the road, a lone blonde figure below waving vigorously beside the listing Rover as I went banking overhead and back towards Lochmo-erantown. I glanced at Cress but she didn't glance back: her eyes were closed. When she did open them a minute later it was to see a red light winking on the panel.

She put on the spare headset hanging beside her seat.

'What does that mean?'

'That we're almost out of juice.'

'So where are we going?'

'There.' I pointed half a mile ahead to where a small building and two pumps were sliding out of the murk.

'An ordinary car filling station; surely you can't.'

I surely could and I surely did, dropping the lever and flaring the nose for quick deceleration and a straight-in approach, at the same time blessing the simplicity of these Highland stations with just their naked pumps set so close to the road. I plonked my skids alongside, one half of the rotor over the centreline and the other over the pumps. A small tubby man came running from the building. I brought the engine to ground idle and the rotor to stop.

'Naem a heavinn mon; what's ye game?' He was as excited as he was indignant, shouting above the scream of the idling Artouste.

I clapped him on the shoulder and shouted back.

'Government business; which is your diesel?'

He pointed to the first pump.

'There, mon, but she's empty. We get delivery the noon.'

Whenever that was it was too late for us. Already the spray crew would be racing after us: they'd seen our direction of flight and knew the ship only had minutes of juice. Not hard to work out where'd we be.

'What about petrol?'

'Oh aye.'

'Good, well stick it in.' Diesel in a turbine was fine but petrol was only for emergencies but this was an emergency.

I grabbed the nozzle from his hand, jammed it in the tank locked open and went back to Cress. 'Try and find a map amongst that lot.' I pointed to the jumble of worksheets, newspapers and tech log down by her feet, at the same time glancing at the fuel gauge: half-full. Tempting to leave it at that and get out but on the theory that the only time you have too much fuel is when you're on fire, I let it flow the full 565 litres. I screwed back the cap. 'Thanks, Jock; send the bill to the government.' He didn't seemed convinced but didn't argue because he'd seen the weapons on the cockpit floor and I was already back aboard and winding the rotor to 100%

'I've found a map.' Cress was holding up a tattered quarter-million from the pile of papers on her lap.

'Good, but hang on, we're lifting off.' I was in a hurry and not least, because I'd already spotted an angry van speeding towards us. This time I'd got the pedals right and pulled away in a climbing turn eastwards that had us nudging the airspeed needle on a hundred knots and our skids on the roof of their cab.

There were other nudgings in the cockpit, not least the jetpipe temperature which was well up in the yellow and a kiss away from red. I knew the reason: petrol burned a lot hotter than kerosene, required lower power settings and halved the life of the engine. I kept the lever up there at max pitch and us trucking eastward.

'Okay, we're about here.' Cress was holding up the map with her finger on a point at the landward end of the loch. I wasn't interested; I was looking instead at the front page of the Scottish newspaper lying folded on her lap. There was a small item of about two single-column inches but in the seconds it took me to read it I knew we'd never be going to Fort William.

'Mike; what are you doing.' She'd dropped the map and was hanging on desperately as I wanged the Llama round in a fifty-degree banked turn that in five juddering seconds had us heading back towards the mouth of Loch Moeran and the open sea beyond.

The last piece of this crazy jigsaw had just slotted into place.

CHAPTER TWENTY-FIVE

'YOU REALLY THINK THIS is what it's all about?'

We were out over the whitecapped depths of the loch-mouth, the grey heaving waters just twenty feet below.

'It has to be. We knew Tracam would need some pretty dramatic act to get the world's attention to his claim and they don't come any more dramatic than this.' I glanced again at the few lines of newsprint that Cress had just finished reading. It was a short report on the District Court proceedings of two days previous but what had gripped my attention was the statement by the Ministry of Defence that henceforth, to avoid further road-convoy fiascos, they would be sending Trident warheads to Scotland by other routes. 'And "other routes" can only mean by sea. That's why the brothers have been supporting the demonstrations against land convoys: they've gambled the MOD would resort to sea transport and it's paid off. Tracam's intelligence would find out when the stuff was sailing and that communications gear in the castle kept track of it. What's the betting that time of 0835 is when the transport will be passing through The Minch and that's where Tracam and his brothers will make their attack. He's not out to highjack a Trident sub; it's the warheads he's after.'

Cress wasn't convinced.

'But the Trident bases are south of here. Surely, if the warheads were being brought by ship they would come *up* the Irish Sea; not around the north of Scotland and *down* through The Minch?'

I thought about that one.

'Perhaps it's a case of avoiding political ramifications with the Irish government. They're uptight enough with British nuclear subs cruising under the Irish Sea; if warheads started going that way too it could cause an even bigger stink.'

'Would anyone know? The whole thing could be done in strictest secrecy.' Cress shook her head again. 'No, there had to be some other reason for sending them round the longer route.'

'And there was…,' I banged my fist on the panel with inspiration, '….the mines; that's what they were for. I bet MOR-RIGAN dropped some in the southern sector of the Irish Sea and then headed back for the English Channel and up the east coast. A few mines floating about would be enough to stop the Trident warheads coming by that route.'

'But we've heard no reports of mines there and, if they did that, why double back instead of heading direct up here to Braedon Isle?'

'Because they needed to land arms at Charlie Smallbright's place on the way and the reason we've heard nothing about mines being found might be the very government secrecy you were talking about. Until the area was swept clear they might feel the less the public knew, the better. What I do know is that Tracam is after those Trident warheads.'

'For what?'

'A bargaining tool probably and we're the only thing that's going to stop him.'

In fact, we'd be staking our lives sooner rather than later. Ahead, another rain-filled storm was sweeping majestically in from The Minch. In seconds we'd be sticking our snouts right into it and the only way I'd keep this basic-instrumented Llama right way up was by keeping its skids on the water and my eyes on the surface.

'But he'll never get away with it. He's crazy.'

'Not crazy, just eccentrically motivated which is what makes him so dangerous. And your wrong on the first bit too: this is something he *could* just get away with but if he doesn't, you can bet he intends the ending will be cataclysmic.'

On my side, out to starboard, Lochmoerantown and the northern headland were fast disappearing in the enfolding murk. Cress's eyes were the other way, towards Braedon Isle and the monastery of Saint Fionn whose misty outlines were just discernible. I let them pass knowing MORRIGAN, Killer, the brothers and their megalomaniac abbot would all be gone and I knew where and for what. As we cleared the loch and started running over tumbling ocean swells, I banked starboard to a new heading of northwest and the rendezvous fifteen miles ahead.

The wind was on the nose now and, with the rattle of split peas on a bass drum, we hit the rain. I stopped my theorising to concentrate on the more immediate problem of keeping us flying and preferably the right way up. The wind at least was stirring the sea and giving me surface reference. I glanced quickly at the clock on the panel: ten minutes to go. Tempting to pull more pitch but the temp gauge was redlining already with that volatile petrol all set to burn the donk for good.

'What do we do when we get there?'

I slid down another ten feet until spray was hitting the helicopter's Plexiglas.

'Hopefully warn them before anything happens.'

'And if we can't?'

She never got an answer to that one because the rain was getting even worse and reference just about gone. I prayed it was the outer edge of the storm and just when I thought it might be my last prayer we burst out into clear air with rain streaming off the windshield and the ships straight ahead.

Visibility was still far from perfect with misty tendrils of drifting stratus clinging to grey spume-swept sea but there was no mistaking MORRIGAN. She was stopped and rolling in the North Minch swell, her main deck a hive of activity as crewmen launched the fast RIBS. There were a dozen commandos in each, all dressed in black wetsuits and yet more boarding Killer's Bolkow, its rotor at 100% and all set for lift-off. Further for'ard, the radar antennae turned relentlessly, providing data on a target we could now see with our naked eyes. I turned to Cress.

'There she is.'

A large vessel was emerging from the mist, a ship with the

lines and deck gear of a freighter but grey-painted and with a helideck over her stern. She was a LSL, a Landing Ship Logistics of the Royal Fleet Auxiliary. As she slipped through the North Minch on that wet October morning, she seemed oblivious to the latent threat just two miles ahead. Cress voiced my thoughts.

'She looks awfully big. Could they really hijack that?'

'Yeh, and they will unless we act fast.'

Even as I said it, I realised that nothing now would be fast enough. From MORRIGAN's helideck, Killer was already lifting off and streaking straight towards the LSL. Tracam had found his quarry and it seemed now that nothing could stop him.

'MIKE, SHE'S TURNING.'

I could see the big LSL healing as her helm was put over and I could see why: MORRIGAN's helicopter was almost on her and the RIBs weren't far behind. I watched as Killer lined up for his spray run on his target, knew his finger was already on the float switch, knew he was all set to dose her with de-vitalizing gas.

It was a simple prelude to boarding what must be a six thousand ton vessel: a good burst of gas over the bridge and any exposed points of resistance and the logistics ship would be easy meat for the twenty-four monastic commandos already enroute to her side unless.....I stuck the nose down and went after the Bolkow.

Even as I did so, the LSL heeled over again in another futile evasion. It wouldn't alter the final result but it did make Killer modify his own approach. Instead of activating the spray, he went banking over the top of the grey leviathan below, turning tighter to get the best angle for his drop, allow for the wind, losing some speed in the process and giving me the chance I needed to get right on his tail. He tightened his turn and I tightened after him and that's when he saw me and knew only one of us was going to come out of this chase alive. Round the LSL we went like a couple of camera aircraft get-

ting their shots of a maiden voyage arrival but there were no
bands playing today and any shots coming from this whirling
formation would be infinitely more lethal.

I'd put him off his first run but how to stop him completely? The Bolkow's rigid rotor made him the more ma-
noeuvrable but we had the lighter load and I could afford to
honk in more bank and turn inside. A couple of more gut-
pulling turns brought us almost alongside. It was close enough
for Killer to look across and recognise me. For a second I
thought he almost smiled but if he did it was because his rear
door was opening slightly with the barrel of a Skorpion coming through the gap. Flashes sparked from its snub nose but
already I was sliding astern and into his blind spot. It would
have been a lucky hit to get us anyway but Killer took my
evasion as momentary superiority, pulled all that was left in
his two Allisons and banked inside me. I rolled in more bank,
pulled more pitch and followed him round.

I glanced across at Cress and saw her face sagging from
the increased G. Then I glanced at our jet-pipe temp: at the
top of the red and all set to vaporise. A great engine, the Artouste and I asked it for just a few more minutes because we
were staying with him, right on his tail and just a little above.
Round and round we went, drifting away from the LSL as we
poled our helicopters just above the sea with blades slapping
and airspeed bleeding and me trying to pull a trick that I was
ashamed to be even thinking.

'Mike, for God's sake,' I didn't blame Cress for screaming,
'we're going to collide.'

'I know; just hang on.'

Killer's Bolkow was filling our windshield now, the jet-
black fuselage seemingly stationary above the fifty-degree
banked sea. A fraction more back-pressure brought me
slightly above him with his rigid-rotor a silver disc just below
our skids. A squeeze more pitch, an imperceptible easing forward of the cyclic and slowly but deathly surely our gear went
forward and down into his staff of life.

The contact, when it came, was as predictable as it was

deadly. Like a rat in a Jack Russell's jaw, our Llama gave a violent shake accompanied by the catastrophic shriek of separating metal. I banked away to starboard, instinctively checking my control response and thanking my guardian angel that it appeared amazingly normal.

The same couldn't be said for Killer and his Bolkow; in fact, nothing about my old antagonist would ever be normal again as his rapidly disintegrating helicopter dropped anvil-like to the sea below. Not that any of the occupants would be knowing anything about it: when those blades came off, the whiplash would have broken their necks quicker than the public hangman.

In life Killer O-Kane had been a bastard but in death he did make one final contribution to humanity. Our crazy dog-fight had drifted us away from the supply ship and over the speeding RIBs. I could see them looking up and manoeuvring wildly to avoid the Bolkow's 5000 pounds of descending spinning death. But a falling helicopter is a pretty unpredictable thing and sometimes it's as easy to speed into it as it is away. The impact, when it came, caught one of the raiders fair and square and it simply disappeared in a welter of flying debris and dismembered humanity. I flew low overhead and felt a ripple of small-arm's fire hit the aircraft. The lost raider's brother was angry, still full of fight and spitting hot lead.

I wheeled quickly out of range, kicked the Llama into wind and brought her into a low hover over the sea.

'Get rid of your door, Cress.'

'Do what?' She was still in a form of shock from our mid-air, scared and confused.

'Jettison the thing....like this.' I transferred the cyclic to my left hand and with the free right slammed down the emergency release. My door fell away into the sea and as it did so I saw the damage done to our own skids. They just weren't there anymore and only a tangle of twisted metal showed where the Bolkow's rotor had thrashed itself to instant death.

It didn't matter; what did was that Cress was hitting the red-painted lever at her side creating a yawning opening where her door had once been. I gave her a thumbs-up, transitioned back into forward flight and yelled.

'Grab the S.M.G., Cress.'

'The what?'

'The gun, for God's sake; pick it up and fire at that other boat.'

'Oh, no.'

'Oh, yes.' The other RIB was heading for the LSL again and still capable of suicidal mischief. I leaned over and grabbed the Skorpion, jammed it into her hands, cocked the lever and pushed the selector to *auto*. 'Just keep that thing pointing outside and zapp them as we go past.' We were running up the raider's churning wake with sparkles of fire coming from her stern. The windshield shattered and there was a cacophony of ripping metal from the bulkhead behind.

I jigged the nose violently to starboard and dived down the boat's side. Another line of neat holes appeared in the Plexiglas just above Cress's head. She looked up, gritted her teeth, said 'You bastards,' and pulled the trigger.

Above the scream of our hot engine, there came the staccato hammer-drill roar of our return fire. I banked away, flinching as I felt more of theirs strike the aircraft.

'You okay, Cress?'

She flashed back a smile and a clenched fist.

'Yeh, but that boat's just had its second-hand value cut by half.'

And its crew too, judging by the number of prostrate forms lying in its bottom. As we chandelled away Cress came back in with a worried look.

'Mike, there's something streaming from the aircraft and I think it's fuel.'

'Strewth!' A glance at the fuel gauge told me how right she was: it was almost empty. One of those rounds had certainly made sure we'd never fly this thing to shore and once again the red light was winking its twelve-minute warning.

I looked for somewhere to land. The LSL had a helideck but putting my skidless helicopter on it was a definite non-starter. Keeping in pitch would keep things upright but when my poor abused engine supped its last globule we'd be rolling over, thrashing ourselves to death and perhaps even the ship we'd tried to save. Besides, these RFA ships were armed and this one would be shooting first and asking second after this morning's melee. Better to ditch alongside. I looked ahead for her grey bulk and saw her steaming away at full speed. I saw something else too and my heart sank again.

Rapidly converging on the LSL was a black hull. MOR-RIGAN; I'd forgotten all about her. During our air fight she'd put on an impressive turn of speed, got ahead of the LSL, and was now turning in towards the logistics ship with intentions hard to mistake.

'Mike, she's going to ram her.'

I didn't answer. I could imagine old Tracam up on the bridge, plans smashed, embittered soul now bent only on revenge, quite prepared to take MORRIGAN to the bottom and the LSL along with her. He could do it too and if my guess as to what that LSL was carrying was correct he'd have alongside him on the seabed the most malignant wreck in the world. Out with a bang in more ways than one and, again, it was down to us to stop him. I banked towards the speeding survey ship, coming in on her starboard quarter.

'You're not going to land?' Cress was already tightening her seatbelt.

'No chance, sweetheart. Jamb that other mag in the gun and get ready for some fancy shooting.'

'At what?'

What indeed: our 7.62 peashooter against 2000 tons of steel ship but a ship with one big weakness.

'Aim for the cable drums, Cress; those big rolls just below the helideck.'

They held over three kilometres of seismic cable each but the important thing was what the cable held: oil, fifty gallons of the stuff for every eighty metres, four thousand gallons in total, highly inflammable and all set to spew if we could just rip the cable. I brought us to a hover right alongside, our belly almost on the water and the rotor a whisker away from the steel supports of the helideck above.

'The full mag, Cress. Right into it.'

She didn't hesitate this time but just let loose a burst steadier than my hover in the turbulent wake of the speeding ship. I hung in there, our rotor almost under the helideck now and wondering just when the engine would quench for ever but shreds were ripping off the cable drums and oil was pouring out. Men were appearing too, at the rail with small arms sparking in our direction. Our instrument panel exploded into a shrapnel of shredding glass and metal and I felt hot scorches across my cheek and arm. Blood was running onto the collective lever; I pulled it up and sent us winging over the helideck to MORRIGAN's port side with Cress changing mags and me yawing the Llama round into a twenty-five knot backward hover.

The aircraft was shuddering like a malarial hypothermic as we exceeded her backward limitations but Cress had a clear field of fire as she gave another full continuous burst into the portside drums. It took half a minute for the crewmen to come clambering over and start loosing off again and by that time their other cable was in shreds and I was winging it astern and out of range.

Through all this, MORRIGAN had not deviated one degree; I could see Tracam himself now, out on the bridge wing, gazing ahead to the LSL drawing closer by the second.

So was our fuel starvation; the gauge had gone the way of the rest of the panel but I knew that we had to be running on fumes. The opposite was the problem on MORRIGAN and I could imagine them running out the hoses, flashing up pumps and trying with all the desperation of doomed men to sluice away that oil. It was time to finish the job.

'The Very pistol, Cress....stick in a cartridge.'

She grabbed the fat-barrelled pistol off the cockpit floor and fumbled in a cartridge as sixty degrees of bank brought us back down MORRIGAN's curving wake and onto her port quarter. I could see why the ship was turning: being so much ahead of the LSL, Tracam could now afford to curve in on his final collision course. He was still on the bridge wing, yelling orders to the crew, directing their fire to keep us from getting closer, half-guessing what would happen if we did. I came on in.

The aircraft twitched and I knew rounds must be hitting the rotor but I waited until all the weapons handlers were on the port side and then wanged us back right over the ship to the starboard quarter. We had about five seconds but there was one gunman remaining on the helideck who'd take far less.

'Now, Cress....right into the oil spill on the cable deck.' She took deliberate aim with both hands and fired but the helideck gunman was firing too and at point-blank range. There was a sudden scream from Cress and an instinctive yank on the cyclic from me as what was left of our windshield shattered into a hundred flying shards. We banked away, sending the pyrotechnic arcing right over the helideck to fall harmlessly still burning into the sea beyond. 'Shit!' I glanced at Cress and saw a rip in the sleeve of her anorak staining an ever-widening red. 'You're hit?'

She gave a brave grin.

'I'm....I'm okay.'

'Can you reload?'

She nodded, broke open the Very, ejected the spent cartridge and pushed in another. She didn't have to ask which; it was the only one left. Only minutes left too; the LSL was filling our vision now as her sleek hull heeled again in another frantic bid to escape the inevitable. I went banking round MORRIGAN's stern, grabbing the Very from Cress as I did so.

We came creaming in, too fast and too close; perhaps it was the awkwardness of flying the thing with my left and holding the pistol with my right or perhaps I just didn't care anymore anyway. Whatever, as more sub-machinegun fire rained down and the cable deck filled the doorless side of my cab, I fired the Very and watched the flare go scorching right to the heart of that oil-soaked cavern. At the same time there were a dozen mind-numbing cracks, a shower of flying metal, a teeth-rattling vibration and I knew our rotor had hit the ship.

We went rolling away to port, not knowing if it was an instinctive control input from me or the searing blast of MORRIGAN's cable deck erupting into a fury of pulsating incandescence. I didn't care either; our abused and shaking helicopter had chosen that second to swallow its last globule of juice. There was a dying whine, a sudden yaw and we hit the sea.

Amidst flying spray I used what control I had left to roll her over to starboard, dig in the rotor and get those scything blades stopped. With her open frame, doorless, screen-less cab and perforated tank the Llama wouldn't be floating for long. I threw off my harness, pushed Cress through the portside opening and by the time I'd scrambled after her the helicopter was gone leaving us kicking and spluttering in its miniscule vortex.

'Mike....MORRIGAN....the other ship.'

I turned in the water and saw our endeavours had all been for nought. MORRIGAN was still forging on at full speed, her blazing stern an inconsequence now and plunging bow, a mere fifty yards from the LSL's vulnerable side. Half a minute would see both ships locked in a catastrophic embrace of doom. I lay still in the water, sick with the futility of it all but the end, when it came, was as unexpected as it was violent.

There was a blinding flash and then a double crack that came pulsing back on shock waves violent enough to jar the very senses out of us. When those senses returned it was to see MORRIGAN already settling and her stern completely gone leaving what was left of that jet-black hull looking like the bloodied stump of a severed arm.

'The mines, Cress....I forgot the two bloody mines.'

I clasped Cress's hand and even then realised my cries of joy might be premature: 2000 tons at twenty knots is a lot of momentum and MORRIGAN was still moving, Kamikaze-like, towards the LSL.

Like a speedboat getting onto the step, so the survey ship's non-existent stern sank lower and lower while her bows rose out of the water, further accentuating the impression of death-throe speed. It was only an impression though; the drag of her pitch was eroding the knots. By the time she reached the LSL she was slow enough for her own quarter wave to catch up, giving the hull one final surfing surge that took it feet from the logistic vessel's swinging stern. The LSL continued round, slowed and then steadied towards us. By now the sea was up to MORRIGAN's wheelhouse, her hull vertical, slipping and sliding ever downward until the grey water closed for ever over her flagless jackstaff and in a cloud of steam, she was gone.

'Finished.' Cress's hand tightened in mine below the surface.

'Yep and for good.'

With the ocean slopping over our heads, we kissed and held each other tight. Engines stopped, the big grey logistics ship came gliding towards us, figures lining the guardrails and a lifeboat already touching the water. Of MORRIGAN, there remained only the wash of her passing and a spreading film of oil, as black as her hull and the habits of the strange sect who'd manned her.

EPILOGUE

ONCE AGAIN THE VENUE was Tower Bridge and once again it was to meet Crestovana Dysart. This time though she was waiting at road level just above the café of our first meeting and I was riding in a chauffeur-driven Daimler that pulled in just long enough for her to squeeze into the back beside me.

'This is rather grand, Captain Tempest. '

We glided smoothly away, the chauffeur taking us around the Tower and joining the flow of traffic westward.

'I guess we've earned it, Cress.' I nodded towards her left arm, still in a sling. 'Healing okay?'

She wrinkled her nose.

'Stitches out in three days. No permanent damage.'

'Good.' I took in her high heels and dark shapely dress. 'You look lovely, Cress.'

She smiled, reached across and, one-handed, rehitched my tie.

'Not so dusty yourself, Mike. '

I squirmed in the first suit I'd worn in years.

'Off the peg at the local store I'm afraid. A long time yet before I'm the pride of Saville Row.'

'You'll do.' She half-turned in her seat and took my hand. 'How did things go at Scotland Yard?'

'All sorted I'm glad to say...' I glanced at my new watch: fifteen minutes to go, '...Special Branch say there'll be no charges on condition...'

Her eyes narrowed.

'... what condition?'

'That we keep absolutely silent about the whole affair; not a word to a soul... ever.'

She gave a little scoff.

'I really don't see how they'll keep all that under wraps.

There's Lady Tracam's kidnap and all those other murders along the way; how are they going to explain those to the media?'

'Standard criminal activity: gang wars, underworld bust-ups.'

'And MORRIGAN's sinking and Sir John Tracam's death?'

'A tragic accident.'

Cress looked at me through cynical eyes.

'Hmmm, they seem to have it all worked out don't they? And you'll go along with that?'

I nodded.

'Yep, with a condition of my own: that they support our claim for the reward from Tracam's insurance and match it from their own coffers.'

'And they agreed?'

'After a bit of haggling... yes.'

She smiled and squeezed my hand.

'Well done, Mike. So we're not coming out of this completely empty-handed.'

I squeezed back.

'Not at all; I figured a quarter-million each should erase a lot of memories.' I lowered my voice slightly. 'I did get them to tell me, though, what they'd found in Tracam's files.'

'Which was...? '

'Mostly what we'd figured ourselves: that MORRIGAN had indeed dropped mines in the Irish Sea. In fact, it was MORRIGAN herself who then reported them.'

Cress's eyebrows did a rise at that one.

'Strange?'

'Not really; remember, they weren't out to sink ships, only ensure that the warheads were diverted around the north of Scotland and through The Minch where the narrow waters made an interception so much more predictable.' I turned and smiled conspiratorially. 'By the way, we were right as regards the secrecy on those mines: the navy sent a minesweeper straight out to sweep them but thought better of making it public knowledge. The Irish Sea was a big enough bone-of-contention without the risk that those mines might have been ours.'

'While never suspecting Sir John Tracam or his ultimate intentions...,' Cress smiled enquiringly, '....which were...?'

'Simply hijack those Trident warheads, take them out into the Atlantic and use them as a bargaining tool...'

'...for us hauling down the Union flag in the north and the Irish government accepting him as king?' Cress sub-consciously rubbed her arm. 'There wasn't really any chance of that was there?'

I shrugged.

'It wasn't totally beyond the bounds of possibility. Nuclear weapons cruising through the Irish Sea has long offended Ireland's sense of neutrality. Tracam striking a blow against that would certainly have won him a lot of support with the Irish people. Special Branch did check his antecedents, by the way.'

'Which were?'

'A genuine line of descent from Cormac MacArt. So, with blood of the old High Kings in his veins and bearing the long-lost crown jewels, he would have had a lot going for him. Indications are that even the republicans would have supported him.'

She raised her eyebrows again.

'I'd have thought that the last thing *Sinn Fein* or the I.R.A. wanted was another monarchy?'

We were paralleling the Thames as the Daimler purred us ever westward.

'Not necessarily. In reality, *Sinn Fein*, the I.R.A. and Tracam's monarchist movement all had the same goal and he might just have been able to achieve it.'

'And if he hadn't... if we'd refused?'

I shrugged again.

'Who knows; megalomaniacs don't often consider the price of failure but if his last actions were anything to go by, he'd doubtless have been prepared to go out with a bang taking those warheads with him. Special Branch investigations have confirmed that he planned to give us an awful lot of agro if we'd even delayed in succumbing to his demands.'

'How?'

'By terrorist action on mainland Britain. Tracam knew the brotherhood weren't big enough to launch a full-blown campaign here and that he needed the support of the I.R.A. In spite of the peace accord there are still cells in this country. Tracam supplied them with those arms we saw landed at the point and the promise of a common goal.'

'A united Ireland?'

'Exactly.'

We were descending into an underpass. Cress sat back in the leather upholstery.

'Phew, what a hornet's nest. Old Tracam didn't seem to mind whom he did business with as long as it was a means to the end. That little weasel Charlie Smallbright was another. Why was he killed then?'

'Simply because he'd fulfilled his purpose. Tracam needed him for his smuggling base and also to handle the kidnap and murder of his wife but his claim to monarchy would only have had support so long as the people never got wind of all the dirty work behind it. If the plan had succeeded, friend Charlie would have been dangerously equipped to start blackmailing. Tracam was no fool and Smallbright had to go and the rest of his gang with him.' We were emerging back into sunlight on the Victoria Embankment. 'Probably the best thing Tracam ever did; the world won't miss scum like Charlie.'

Falling astern on our left was a bridge: Blackfriars. It was a name to conjure a myriad of emotions and in Cress too, judging by her next question.

'What about our dedicated order of Saint Fionns? Did any of them survive?'

I shook my head.

'No, lost to a man with MORRIGAN.'

She looked sad.

'Presumably taking the Irish crown jewels with them.'

The Thames was sparkling in the pale winter sun but I knew Cress's thoughts were in far deeper waters. 'That regalia certainly seems to have carried its own curse on all who touched it. Stolen, lost for nearly a century, then found and then lost again. A pity really because they sounded so beautiful and now I'll never get to see them.'

'I'm not so sure.'

Her look of sadness was replaced by one of intrigue.

'Go on?'

I winked knowingly.

'Word is that a certain person is secretly negotiating with the Irish department of antiquities for the regalia's restoration to Dublin Castle.' I smiled at her bewildered expression. 'I'll give you a clue: she's peroxide blonde and currently driving a slightly battered Range Rover.'

Cress gasped.

'Lena LeVoy, the little tar....negotiator.' She sat back, chuckling. 'Well, good for Lena. I thought she was keen to keep hold of that habit she escaped in. When did she grab them?'

'Apparently in the few minutes after my escape from the loo. Tracam had gone in himself, found the window open and in the confusion of raising the hue and cry, left the regalia on his desk. Lena decided it was a good time to make her break, saw the jewels and devised her own separation settlement.'

Cress shook her head.

'So Lena gets the millions for recovering the jewels.' She took a couple of seconds to let the irony of that sink well in before smiling philosophically. 'Well I'm pleased they were saved and going back to where they belong.'

I wasn't so sure we were going to where we belonged. The Embankment was swinging south now with the London Eye across the river and Big Ben and Westminster coming into view ahead. Atop parliament, the Union flag stirred lazily in the fickle breeze. Cress nodded towards it.

'And our government have been spared the embarrassment of losing a big chunk of their nuclear arsenal.'

I nodded.

'And very grateful they are too.' Big Ben was looming over us now, its hands five minutes short of the hour. The chauffeur swung us right and I felt myself subconsciously adjusting my tie. 'That's why he wants to see us; to thank us personally.'

She looked cynical.

'And cement our silence. Well, he's not going to find me very silent at our meeting. I'm going to tell him just what I think of Trident warheads and the rest of his death machine.'

I groaned inwardly as we rounded Parliament Square, almost a full circumnavigation before we swung left into Parliament Street.

'Don't bite the hand, Cress.' I nodded towards the Treasury just sliding by on the left. 'They're the ones who are going to secure my silence.'

She laughed.

'Don't worry, I'll go easy on him.' Parliament Street merged into Whitehall and her expression slipped slightly. 'What are your plans now, Mike?'

'Get another job, I expect.'

'Well that shouldn't be too difficult now you've got friends in high places.' We were slowing and turning left before some large ornamental gates. Police guards checked our names with the chauffeur against a list on a clipboard and then the gates swung open and we glided through. Cress gave my hand another squeeze. 'Nervous?'

I shrugged as nonchalantly as the sense of the occasion would allow.

'Surviving, but I could do with a cigarette.'

She gave a mock frown.

'Well, you can forget that, Mike Tempest; you promised, remember?'

I did and wondered if one day Crestovana Dysart would allow me to make yet more promises.

Ahead, a raised barrier in the roadway prevented further

progress. More coveralled guards checked beneath the Daimler with detection lights, the barrier retracted back into the
roadway and we glided ahead the few yards to in front of the
door. The chauffeur got out and I turned to the slim figure
beside me.

'Well, here we are.'

Cress smiled'

'Yes, and it's been quite a journey.' Her expression deep-
ened slightly. 'Mike, about that reward...'

My eyes narrowed, cynically.

'What about it?'

She smiled again.

'Instead of splitting it, why don't we just put it into a joint
account.'

I beamed.

'As soon as you like, Miss Dysart.'

With no more words, I helped her out and, hand-in-
hand, we went up to the big black door with the brass 10. Perhaps Cress was stretching things a bit when she called them
"friends" but she was right on the second bit: places didn't
come much higher than this.

The door opened and we went inside.

AUTHOR'S NOTE

THIS STORY IS, OF course, fiction but not *pure* fiction. The background crime, the theft of the Irish Crown Jewels from Dublin Castle in 1907, really did happen. The suspects named were those sought by Scotland Yard at the time, though no charges were ever brought to bear. Dublin Castle still stands in all its grandeur and, within it, the Bedford Tower, scene of one of the great, but little known, unsolved mysteries of the twentieth century.

For more information, visit *www.chriscrowther.co.uk*

Printed in the United Kingdom
by Lightning Source UK Ltd.
119003UK00002B/70-699